Petals Between the Pages

A BEAUTY AND THE BEAST RETELLING

ONCE UPON A FAIRYTALE

SERENE HEINER

CARPE VITAM
PRESS LLC

One

R idge splayed his fingers, letting the damp fall air pour through them as he drove down the county highway. The reception was poor on this stretch of road so he'd turned off the staticky radio and rolled down the window. The quiet was a blessing and curse. He'd learned long ago it was never good to be left alone with his own thoughts for too long.

Ahead, a splash of color caught his eye. He slowed, pulling his old beater truck off to the side of the road, and parked behind the flashy, bright yellow sports car. A man in a dark sweater and jeans paced back and forth, yelling into his cell phone.

"Can you hear me now?" the man said, as though screaming the words would somehow help with the connection.

Ridge sighed as he climbed out of his truck. "Why do they always say that?"

It wasn't cold exactly, but here in the shade of the tall

trees that canopied both sides of the highway, there was a definite chill in the air.

Ridge's boots crushed on the loose gravel of the road's shoulder and the man glanced at him then stuck a finger in his ear as though the noise was too much. Ridge barely managed to refrain from rolling his eyes when he read the word BEAST in thick black letters on the license plate. Someone thought a lot of himself.

"No," the man shouted. "I pay good money for your service. Hello? No, you have ten minutes to get here or I'm canceling my account and going somewhere else!" He hung up and swore.

Ridge leaned against his truck as the man spun around to face him. He jolted. Even though he didn't exactly recognize the guy, especially with the tacky sunglasses that seemed way too big for his face, Ridge knew exactly who he was.

Only one family had the kind of money that allowed for such a useless luxury as this car and they only had one son. Milton Freewater. A boy who'd been sent away to "study abroad" after elementary school. But really, everyone knew Milton's father thought his son deserved better than a "simple" public school education. During the summers, the family traveled so Ridge hadn't seen him in years.

"What do you want?" Milton barked.

Ridge shrugged, not at all surprised Milton didn't recognize him. "Nothing. I was just wondering if you'd like some help changing your flat." He indicated to the puddle of rubber that used to be a tire.

Milton shook his head. "Not necessary. Someone will

be—better be—here in ten minutes to take care of it." He opened his car door and started rummaging through the glove compartment.

Ridge pushed away from the grill and walked up behind him. The car sure was flashy, with its almost blinding paint job and nearly black tinted windows. But so tiny. It made him think of a bumble bee. He felt claustrophobic just thinking about having to sit inside that thing.

He glanced over Milton's head. Even the back seat that held two twenty pound propane tanks seemed almost useless. Where did passengers put their legs? It felt like a waste. He tried not to think about how much the car cost and how that amount of money would help get him and his mom back on their feet.

"I can get you on the road in less time than that," Ridge offered.

Milton jumped, clearly not expecting Ridge to be standing right behind him. He straightened and slammed his door shut.

"I said no."

Ridge held up his hands. "Fine." He spun back to his truck and pulled open the squeaky door. "Still the same ole' prick," he muttered.

* * *

Ridge killed the truck's engine, leaving the keys jangling in the ignition, and stared at the blue paint peeling off his front door. The porch dropped a little on the left side and one of the shutters had fallen off. He sighed. It needed so much work, but it required time he didn't have and repairs he couldn't afford.

He pulled the little orange bottle of prescription pain pills from his coat pocket and rolled it between his fingers.

He should tell Mom he couldn't find any. He should say it was time to get help. Maybe he would. Maybe today, he could finally do it.

Tucking the pills back into his pocket, Ridge finally stepped into the pine-scented air. It was so still. He missed Dutchess, his dad's old hunting dog. At least she'd always been happy to see him.

Ridge glanced up. There should have been smoke curling from the wood stove chimney, but everything was quiet.

A curl of ice wound its way through his chest. He raced toward the house and leapt onto the porch, clearing the steps altogether, and pushed open the door.

The interior was dark and dusty, with the faint smell of an unwashed body hovering in the air.

"Mom?" he called, his heart thudding. He flipped the lightswitch but the room stayed dark. He swore under his breath. He'd put payment for the electric bill in the mail before he'd left—

His gaze fell to a crumpled envelope beside the garbage can. Smoothing it out, he sighed as he read his own handwriting and the address of the power company. He didn't normally pay in cash but there hadn't been enough in the bank so he'd used money from a repair job he'd done for someone in town.

"That explains the lights," he muttered and rubbed

his eyes. He knew better than to leave extra cash anywhere near Mom, but he'd been in a hurry and hadn't dropped the money off himself. Rookie mistake.

The living room was cold, with a pile of rumpled blankets and an empty pizza box on the coffee table. In the kitchen, open peanut butter and jelly jars stood next to an open bag of bread, no doubt stale now. Dirty dishes cluttered the sink and counters.

"Mom?" he yelled again, heading back to the bedrooms. He paused just outside her half open door. His pulse quickened. What would he find on the other side?

Maybe she'd finally overdosed. With that single thought, so many emotions threatened to steal his breath. He loved his mother. Sometimes it was just... hard.

Ridge pushed open the door, which gave a high-pitched creak in protest. "Mom?" he said again, this time quietly.

There was a small lump under the dingy sheets of the bed. Silently, he moved to the other side.

Empty pill bottles lay scattered on the nightstand—more than she needed. His gaze shifted to his mom's face and he leaned in close. She was breathing.

At least there was that. Tension slid from his shoulders.

He slipped from the room and went back into the kitchen, checking the refrigerator and pantry. Both were pretty bare.

"Guess you didn't use the money I did leave for you on groceries," he said out loud, just to break up the repressive silence.

A deep exhaustion pulled at him, but there was too much to do. First, he'd get a fire going, then go into town, pay the power bill, and pick up some groceries. He'd unload the truck when he got back.

It wasn't long before the crackle of burning wood and its warmth began to fill the room. Ridge jotted down a quick note that he was back in case his mom happened to wake up.

Outside, he pulled the tarp off his old motorcycle and for the first time, he smiled. It wasn't anything grand but he wouldn't have traded it for the world. Besides being cheaper to drive than the gas-guzzling truck, it was the closest he came to freedom.

Ridge cranked the kick starter and the engine roared to life. He eased into the seat, feeling the hum of the engine through his core. Glancing back at the house, his smile faded. More than once he'd been tempted to drive away and just... keep going.

He revved the engine and faced the road. No, his mom needed him, and if he were being honest, there was also one other person holding him here.

Tearing out of the driveway, he headed toward town.

Bear River was your typical small town and had the basic necessities: a bank, a grocery store, two gas stations on opposite ends, one school for both elementary and junior high, a high school, and a library. Most people were born and raised here, never leaving, satisfied to stay in the bubble they'd created and ignore the outside world.

Everything was quaint and picture perfect, like a Hollywood movie. Pretty on the outside but behind the scenes, it was a different story.

Never leaving this place gave the community nothing to talk about but each other. Ridge knew about that more than most. Sometimes, it was suffocating.

He stopped at the power station and paid the electric bill, glaring at the receptionist, a teenager working after school hours by the looks of it, until she promised the power would be turned back on before she left that day.

"Thank you," he muttered, not caring if she actually heard him or not.

Ridge slid his way through the grocery store, keeping his sunglasses on and his head down. He could handle the whispers his presence seemed to generate; he'd been used to that since the Brambette twins and their best friend, Charlotte, spread rumors about him in high school, rumors he didn't bother to contradict. What was the point? Everyone would believe the "well-bred" girls over the poor, mannerless boy from the wrong side of town anyway.

He moved to the checkout stand, keeping a safe distance between him and Mrs. Potts, who was twittering softly to Mrs. Whitter, an old crone who couldn't talk quietly if her life depended on it.

"Yes!" Mrs. Potts said, clapping her hands together. "I have seen him. The CEO of Stoneworks Industries. He turned out quite handsome, don't you think?" She lowered her voice but Ridge heard every word. "No doubt attending school abroad has cultured him in plenty of interesting ways."

Mrs. Whitter cackled and elbowed her. "I wouldn't mind a sample of that European culture myself, if you know what I mean."

Mrs. Potts turned red and giggled, then said something Ridge blessedly couldn't hear. He had zero interest in the town gossip. He'd heard his own name passed around far too often and it was rarely good.

Mrs. Whitter burst out an abrupt laugh. "If that girl isn't just melting into a puddle all over her books then she's a bigger fool than I thought!"

This caught Ridge's full attention. He tried to inch closer without drawing attention but Mrs. Potts noticed him then. Her eyes widened, her gaze flicking over him from head to toe.

Ridge glanced down at himself. His dirty jeans were ripped in a few places, but not in the cool way that was all the rage. He'd actually earned those holes the old fashioned way—working. After a week tromping through the mountains, his muddy boots could stand to be wiped off and his flannel shirt, which was unbuttoned and draped over a black, mud splattered shirt, was missing a couple snaps.

Ridge frowned. Maybe he should have changed first. He probably smelled worse than he looked, and that was saying something.

Snatching up their shopping bags, the two women hurried from the store.

With a sigh, Ridge stuffed his few groceries into the saddle bags, cursing the headache building behind his eyes.

There was only one girl they could be talking about so he steered his bike toward the tiny bookstore on the edge of town.

Two

Ridge glanced at the time on his phone. The bookstore was already closed for the day, but only barely. He sped up.

As he took the corner, Ridge's heart beat faster, the way it always did when the tiny shop came into view. It was an old, brick building with nothing but acres of open land behind it.

When the mayor decided they needed a new town hall, one that was actually *in* town, he sold the building and the property it sat on to Isobelle's father before she was even born. She'd mentioned once it cost his whole inheritance and savings. Ridge didn't know how many acres it was but the land went all the way to the river.

In front of the bookstore stood two figures. One was a tall, broad-shouldered man, with light hair, wearing a dark sweater and jeans.

Ridge stopped the bike.

Milton.

The other figure was shorter, with long brown hair tied back with a blue ribbon.

Isobelle.

Ridge's stomach flipped, the way it always did when he saw her. Somehow, it never stopped.

At the sound of his motor, both figures turned in his direction. He should keep going, he shouldn't care that Milton was with Isobelle, but he found himself pulling up beside them and killing the engine.

There was an awkward pause as the three of them just looked at each other.

"Uh, hi, Ridge," Isobelle finally said.

Even though he'd only been gone a week, the sound of her voice sent goosebumps shooting down his arms. He nodded at her, ignoring the way Milton started when she said Ridge's name. He suddenly felt foolish and wished there was a way he could just up and drive away without making himself look like a total idiot.

When he didn't say anything, Isobelle's eyes flicked from Ridge to Milton as though she sensed something was off. "How was your trip?"

"Good," Ridge managed to say, but for some reason he couldn't string any more words together. He wanted to tell her all about the rich Frenchman who'd hired him as a guide for his hunting trip, but words refused to come.

Isobelle was starting to look uncomfortable now, which made Ridge kind of hate himself.

"Uh, you remember Milton Freewater, right?" she finally asked.

Ridge forced his eyes to the man beside her.

Milton's wide smile was blindingly white, making

Ridge wonder if there was any tooth bleach left in the world.

"Of course," he said, and shook Milton's outstretched hand. Neither one mentioned their earlier encounter.

Ridge's tanned skin looked extra dark against Milton's. He drew his hand back quickly, hating that he noticed how dirty his own were in comparison to Milton's soft, clean ones.

"Ridge Larsen," Milton said with a slight accent that Ridge was sure hadn't been there before. "Wow, you've sure changed! Last time I saw you you were just a scrawny kid in ripped pants." His eyes darted down to Ridge's jeans and laughed. "Well, I guess some things haven't changed a bit."

Milton's laugh was full and rich, the kind of laugh women seemed to like. Ridge glanced at Isobelle. She was watching him, a wide smile on her face. It was clear she liked his laugh. Ridge's stomach tightened.

"But seriously, man," Milton said. "You're huge! You'll have to tell me your workout routine and your tips for bulking up." He flexed a massive bicep of his own.

"Lots of eggs," Ridge deadpanned, unintentionally making Milton laugh his stupid laugh again. He wasn't lying about the eggs. When he was a teenager they had a few chickens and there were many, many times the only thing they had to eat were the eggs they laid. Especially those first few months after his dad left.

Ridge turned his attention back to Isobelle and away from his memories. "How was your week?"

She shrugged, clutching a book in her arms, like she

was upset but also... not. Ridge couldn't help but notice it was a book he'd seen her with a dozen times—a medieval romance and her favorite story of all time. When he found out it was her favorite, he'd read it too.

More than once.

Ridge gave her a measured look and she sighed.

"Well, Dad is sick again," she said. "The doctor's are worried about his lungs this winter." She bit her lip, drawing Ridge's gaze. He drew in a slow breath, trying not to stare.

Then Milton wrapped an arm around her shoulders and Ridge fought the urge to throat punch him. "It's alright, darling. Retirement will be just the thing he needs to finally rest and relieve some stress from his life."

Darling? "Retire?" Ridge focused on Isobelle. "But that would leave just you running the bookshop."

She nodded, her face pinched. But then she brightened. "Oh! I forgot to tell you!" She placed a hand on Milton's arm. "And you! I heard back from Gabrielle Villeneuve."

Ridge leaned forward. "And?" It was all she'd talked about before he'd left. How she'd reached out to her favorite author, inviting the woman to make Isobelle's little shop a stop for a signing event on her tour. Ridge really only understood about half of what that actually meant.

Her face split into a wide smile. "She said yes!" Isobelle did a little dance and Ridge couldn't stop his mouth from curving up. It was unfair of her to be so adorable.

"I still can't believe it!" Isobelle beamed. "Gabrielle is

going to come to *my* bookstore! This will put me on the map!"

Now, Ridge was fully smiling, not only at the way she practically floated on air, but at the way Milton looked utterly confused.

"I've already placed a rather large order for her new book." At this, she cringed. "I hope we get a good turnout. I need to be able to sell them all."

"I'm sure it will be a huge success," Milton piped in then.

Ridge's smile faded. Why was he still here?

But Isobelle smiled at the twit. "Thank you! I hope so too because I'd really like to add on a little coffee shop."

"That sounds wonderful, darling," Milton chimed in, making Ridge wonder how bad it would be if he broke the guy's perfect nose.

"I'm sure your little adventure will be marvelous." Milton took Isobelle's hand. "But, if it doesn't work out..."

Ridge looked from him to Isobelle, who seemed suddenly deflated.

"What?" he asked.

Milton cut him a sharp look. "Well, I've been trying to convince this beautiful lady to sell the shop to Stoneworks Industries but she has her heart set on making it a grand success." He smiled down at her like she was a chihuahua in a handbag.

Ridge blinked. What the hell? He'd only been gone a week! When had this guy shoved his way into such familiarity with her?

13

"What?" This time, the word came out in a sharp bark, making Isobelle flinch.

Ridge just stared. There was no way she'd consider it. That place was her life.

Isobelle looked down at her feet.

Ridge felt his hackles rise as he looked between them both. "Izzy, what's going on?"

He knew he had no right to ask, but what could possibly make her consider such an outrageous move?

"Don't you think that's personal?" Milton said and put an arm around Isobelle's shoulders again.

"No, it's okay," Isobelle said. "Ridge and I had talked a little bit about it already."

Milton's face darkened but his smile was wide. "Whatever you wish."

Isobelle looked at Ridge. "We already have a lot of medical bills and with Dad getting worse..." She shrugged. "The bookstore doesn't sell much."

Her unspoken words hung in the air. Her shop wasn't making enough money to pay the expenses. That was a huge strain Ridge completely understood.

"Why doesn't Stoneworks host..." Ridge waved his hand in the air like an idiot, reaching for words that weren't there. "A fair or... something. To bring in people. There's other ways to help the bookstore. You don't need to sell it," he said, folding his arms across his chest, glaring at Milton, daring the guy to make fun of how foolish he sounded.

The pretty boy in perfect jeans sighed. "That's just a bandaid for a bullet hole option. Even if Stoneworks did host *'something'* —his eyes cut to Ridge— "as you so eloquently stated, it doesn't solve the issue of her father's growing bills, nor will it create a steady income for her." He gave Isobelle's shoulders a squeeze. "But maybe bringing this author to your little store will change things."

Ridge imagined dragging his keys through some bright yellow paint.

"And if it doesn't..." Milton shrugged. "Look, I'm just trying to help. It's something for you to think about, anyway. And with the extra money, you could finally travel. Go have adventures in the great wide somewhere."

Isobelle smiled up at him, though it didn't reach her eyes. "Thank you, that's very sweet."

Ridge fisted his hands, squeezing them so hard it hurt. Izzy had always wanted to see the places she read about in her books, real or imagined.

"I'll think about it. Truly," she said softly.

"That's my girl," Milton said, and pressed a kiss into her hair.

Ridge nearly tipped over his bike. *His* girl?

Then, Mr. Perfect-white-teeth pulled a buzzing phone from his pocket. It could have been Ridge's imagination, but it looked like Milton's face paled.

"Uh, I need to go. I'll see you tomorrow, darling."

Then he looked at Ridge. "It was good to see you again." He held out his hand. This time, Ridge did not shake it.

After an awkward moment, Milton withdrew his hand and sauntered to his stupid yellow car with its stupid license plate.

Ridge had stopped comparing himself to people a

long time ago, but in this moment he felt like poor, dirty trash. Just like his own father used to call him.

He wanted to ask Isobelle a million things: was she dating this guy? When did it start? She wouldn't really sell the bookstore, would she? But one look at her hunched shoulders and he swallowed all his questions.

"You okay?"

She shrugged one shoulder. "To be honest, I don't want to talk about it right now."

"Not even about the author?"

Isobelle's eyes lifted to watch Milton's car disappear and slowly shook her head.

Ridge ground his teeth.

She finally met his eyes and immediately, Ridge's heart raced.

"Tell me about your trip," she said. "Not the hunting part, but you mentioned before you left you were taking a Frenchman?"

Ridge blinked, his brain trying to switch gears. Then, he relaxed. This was what he'd come for. This was what he'd wanted to do from the moment he got back, and he wouldn't let that prick steal it from him. It was all he had.

Nodding, Ridge got off his bike, moving to sit on the bench set up outside the bookstore. Someone called Isobelle's name from across the street and she waved.

Ridge felt a familiar warmth fill his chest. Despite how dirty he looked or how poor his family was, and despite the rumors that had swirled around him his whole life, Isobelle never seemed embarrassed to be seen with him, nor called any attention to his flaws. She'd never treated him as "less than." She had no idea how much that meant to him.

"You would have liked him," Ridge said, as Isobelle took a seat beside him. Now he really wished he'd taken the time to shower first. "His name was Cogsworth."

Isobelle choked, smiling. "You're making that up."

Ridge shook his head. "I'm totally not. He parted his hair right down the middle and had a mustache that even curled up at the ends."

At this, she laughed and the knot on Ridge's chest loosened. He could listen to that all day.

This had been one of Ridge's most profitable trips. Cogsworth had paid well and gave him the meat from the elk they'd managed to bag as a tip. It would feed him and his mom through the winter and he'd be able to sell off the rest.

He told Isobelle about the fancy tea set the man had brought along and tried to use, about how he hadn't packed enough warm clothes, and the way his accent made him pronounce the word clothes like "clofs."

Isobelle's attention was all on him, her whole face bright and expressive as she drank in every detail Ridge could remember about the foreigner. Her desire for travel and yearning for adventure was clearly evident on her face. It had become a tradition between them—him telling her about the strange people he met as a hunting guide and her asking question after question about them and their mannerisms. Sometimes she would look up the places they'd come from and study their culture.

This. This was his favorite thing to do in the entire world and he wanted to do it forever.

Pieces of brown hair blew into her face as they talked and Ridge almost reached up to brush them away. Then he remembered his dirty hands and old clothes that looked quite out of place beside Isobelle's light blue top and dark jeans.

Ridge looked at the book in her lap, a book he'd read because she loved it so much. On the cover, a prince with fair hair and bright blue eyes held a woman with flowing brown hair. They looked like Milton and Isobelle.

Then his phone buzzed. He glanced at it—Mom.

The lightness in him died as reality slapped some sense back into him. Ridge had nothing to offer her. Nothing except poverty, hardship, and a pill-addicted mother-in-law.

He should get home, take care of her. Take care of the elk meat, take care of the dying garden, haul away the weeks of garbage buildup, and a dozen other things. The list went on and on and on.

Isobelle sensed the change in him and her smile faded too.

"I better go," he muttered. Isobelle didn't say anything as he stood and strode back to his bike. Everyone in town assumed his mom was always sick and that ever since Dad left after her alleged accident, it was hard for her to make it into town.

No one knew the truth, and if he was careful, Isobelle would never find out. Pity was the last thing he wanted from her.

He glanced at her, only to find her still on the bench, watching him with an expression he couldn't quite read.

Swallowing hard, Ridge drove away without saying goodbye.

Three

Ridge woke with a start, staying still out of habit, listening. There—another slight scraping noise. Someone was definitely in his room.

Dad. Slowly, he gripped the handle of the baseball bat he kept between his pillows and the headboard. Switching on his lamp, he jumped to his feet and spun.

There was a small gasp and the hazy blob came into focus.

"Mom?"

She hovered over his nightstand like an apparition, all gaunt cheekbones and sunken eyes ringed with dark smudges.

He lowered the bat. "What are you doing?" he asked, even though he already knew the answer. "It's three in the morning."

She didn't usually wake him up. In fact, she was rarely up before him.

"Uh—I'm sorry," she said, straightening and

smoothing her hands on her dirty sweats. "I didn't mean to wake you, I was just... I was—"

"Looking for pills?"

Her face flushed. "My knee has been hurting really bad all night and I was hoping to get some chores done tomorrow so I wanted to be able to sleep."

Ridge didn't move.

She shifted, her eyes still searching the room. "It's just...hard to sleep, so I figured if I could just take the edge off...."

Holding in a sigh, Ridge rubbed his eyes. It was always a slight variation of the same story, the same reasons, the same excuses. His eyes cut to his coat. The painkillers he'd picked up in Tuscal City were still there. They had to be if she was searching.

"Mom, you should still have some from before I left on my trip. There were plenty."

Her eyes filled with tears. "I know, but I fell while you were gone and I landed wrong and it just hurt so bad I could hardly think straight."

Shaking his head, Ridge struggled with his warring guilt and frustration. It was always the same song and dance. This had to stop. She needed help.

Drawing in a deep breath, he said the words before either one of them could talk him out of it. "Listen, Mom. I think it's time to see someone about this." He raised his eyes to hers. "You have a problem."

She reared back like he'd slapped her. "I do not. You —you don't know what it's like, to always be in pain, to relive that memory over and over every time you close my eyes. To jump at every noise, wondering if he's come back."

But Ridge did know. He knew exactly what she was talking about, but it didn't change the fact that the substance abuse had grown worse over the years.

"Mom," he tried, keeping his voice soft, just like he would with an injured animal. "You can't stayed cooped up in this house—-"

"What would you know, anyway?" she yelled, her eyes glistening with tears and bright with rage. "You're always gone, galavanting through the woods with fancy folk from all over the world, while I sit at home, struggling to survive the pain, barely able to take care of myself!"

Her words were like a knife to his chest, anger and hurt spilling from the wound. Did she really not see that he was trying to help them survive?

"Don't turn this on me," he said, struggling to keep his voice even. "Being a hunting guide is good pay. It's what covers the bills and keeps food on the table—"

"Oh sure," she snarled. "You're going to throw that in my face, are you? How you do all the work and I'm totally worthless? How—how I'm pathetic and... and stupid?"

Ridge's gut twisted and he reached out a hand to her, hating that Dad's words still held so much power over her. "Mom, that's not what I—"

She took an awkward step back. Tears spilled down her cheeks as her lip curled. "What? You gunna shove me down the stairs too? Break my other leg?"

This time, Ridge felt her words like a physical blow, and he'd received plenty at the hands of his dad. He would never hit a woman. He would *never* be like his dad, who'd run off just before Mom was released from the hospital.

Something in his expression must have shown his hurt because his mom covered her mouth and stumbled from the room.

Swallowing bile, Ridge pulled on a shirt and went after her. "Mom!" He ran into the living room just as there was a wall-shaking *bang,* like a distant explosion. For a moment, he stopped in his tracks. It didn't sound super close but—

Bang. Another one.

He ran through the living room and pulled open the front door. A faint glow backlit the treeline and above it, smoke. Lots of it. "What the—"

"It's gotta be somewhere in town, but I can't tell what it would be," Mom whispered from behind him, their fight momentarily forgotten.

It only took Ridge a minute to grab his boots and keys. He paused, then went back to his room and snatched his coat with the pills still in the pocket.

"Stay here," he said as he raced past his mom. "I'll go see what's happening."

Ridge revved the engine of his motorcycle and sped out of the driveway, gravel and dirt spraying from beneath the back wheel.

As he drew closer to town, the wails of sirens grew louder until they were piercing. Heart hammering, Ridge headed toward the pillar of smoke. Turning a corner, his stomach twisted into a painful knot. Isobelle's bookstore.

He weaved through cars and emergency vehicles until he found an alley where he ditched his bike. Then, he was running, shoving his way through the massive crowd of gawking townsfolk that was quickly getting bigger.

He pushed toward the fire. What if she had stayed the night there? Sometimes she did. She could be trapped inside! She could already be—

"Hey!" someone yelled when he shouldered them out of the way, but Ridge didn't stop to see. He was focused ahead, scanning faces for familiar brown eyes, searching heads for a wisp of blue ribbon. His chest hurt from the beating his heart was giving it.

"Izzy," he finally yelled, turning in a circle. Everything was a blur, a dizzying mass of smoke and flame and worried faces. But none of them were hers. "Isobelle," he breathed, searching... searching.... His breath hitched. A girl wrapped in a blanket stood staring at the flames, her eyes wide and luminous, tears running silently down her cheeks while the sheriff stood beside her, asking questions.

Ridge shoved through the people eating up the space between them.

"Izzy!" he yelled again, and this time she moved her eyes from the flames to meet his. His heart wrenched at the hollow, haunted look in them. For the briefest moment, a tiny light flared in their depths, like she was glad he was there.

Isobelle opened her mouth.

He was almost to her.

Then, a body stepped between them, blocking his view.

"Oh, Isobelle," Milton said, grabbing her arms. "I

24

came as fast as I could." He gathered her to him and Ridge stopped dead in his tracks.

"I'm here. I'm here now," Milton crooned, smoothing Isobelle's hair. "Give us a moment, would you, Sheriff?"

Ridge wanted to break his fingers.

"Everything will be alright, I'm here now. I'll take care of you."

Ridge shoved his fists into his jacket pockets. Prick or no prick, he wanted to see Isobelle.

"What happened?" Ridge snapped, his words coming out harsher than he'd meant them.

Milton turned, still holding Isobelle tight to his chest. She didn't fight him, just... leaned on him, like she might collapse.

Milton's face turned to a scowl. "Obviously her beloved bookstore is in flames."

Ridge inhaled a slow breath. How bad would punching this guy be, really?

"I meant," he said between clenched teeth, "do you know *why* it's in flames?"

Isobelle eased herself back from Milton, an occasional tear still sliding down her cheeks. She shook her head. "It's too early to know."

Firefighters were shooting water at the licking flames but it was clear the old building was gone.

He wanted to talk to Isobelle *alone* but Milton was still hovering, touching her, whispering over and over that he would take care of her.

"We'll help you rebuild, with the insurance money," Ridge blurted and immediately regretted his words. It was too soon to say something like that. He didn't know how much insurance would pay out or if it would be enough to buy new books.

For a moment, Isobelle looked at him with such heart-wrenching hope and appreciation, then her eyes dimmed and darkened, as though she could hear his own thoughts.

"Even if we did, it would never get done in time for the book tour," Isobelle whispered.

Ridge glanced at Milton. Of course he was about to swoop in and save the day and become the hero by offering to build her a bigger, better bookstore in only a week's time. He hated him.

Milton sighed. "Darling, think of this as a blessing in disguise. You can sell me the land. I mean, it's pretty worthless at this point but I'm sure my father would be willing to pay more than it's worth. Then, with the money, you and your dad could travel and see the world!" He gripped her arms again. "Just think of it! All the places you read about you could actually go see! Wouldn't it be wonderful?"

Ridge just stared. Seriously? That's what he was going to offer her? He had all the money in the world and he wasn't offering to help her rebuild?

Isobelle didn't say anything for a long while, just turned back to the flames. "I'll talk to Dad."

Ridge ground his teeth. She couldn't seriously be thinking about it. This land, and the bookstore, was supposed to be her future, a future she wanted.

"Izzy," Ridge said, taking a step toward her. "You don't have to—"

"I don't exactly have a lot of options, do I?" she snapped, then disappeared into the crowd.

Ridge went to go after her but Milton said, "Why are you making this worse for her?"

That pulled him up short. "What is that supposed to mean?"

"I mean," Milton said, "she's just lost everything and now you're telling her not to do the one thing that can save her and her father from drowning in debt? Do you want her to have to file for bankruptcy?"

Ridge leaned forward, "Why don't you just offer to build a new shop?" He couldn't believe he was suggesting this moron be her hero, but if it meant Isobelle would be happy he wouldn't be the one to stand in the way. "You have more money than you need. I bet it would be like buying a dollhouse."

Milton shook his head. "It's not up to me. My father controls all the money and he's already made it perfectly clear he has no interest in putting his money on a sinking ship. No one goes to bookstores anymore, no one wants books. Everyone just reads stuff on their phones anyway."

He looked in the direction Isobelle had disappeared. "I'm trying to do what's best for her." Then he too moved into the darkness, leaving Ridge to watch the fire alone.

Four

The fire finally burned itself out, leaving nothing but piles of charred brick. Even now, three days later, it still smelled of ash and smoke, and... something else. Ridge stared at it, wishing with everything in him he could do something for Isobelle, have some way to change what had happened.

But he was a nobody with no money and nothing to offer. He hadn't seen Isobelle since the fire. She wouldn't answer his calls and her texts were short assurances that she was alright, but he'd seen Milton's yellow car parked outside her house a couple times.

Ridge had felt low plenty of times, pathetic even, especially when his dad would smack Mom or him around, but never in his life had he felt so completely and utterly useless.

He clutched the book he'd brought from his house. It was his own copy of the same book she'd been holding when he got back from his trip. He found out later she'd put it back inside the store after he'd driven away and it had burned along with all the others.

Ridge parked his motorcycle in a cluster of trees a couple blocks away from Isobelle's house. He tucked the book under his arms and walked through the thick foliage growing on either side of the path. Some thorns of a wild, late-blooming rosebush snagged his clothes and when he pulled away, petals from the flowers scattered to the ground.

He stopped, staring at their deep red color. Once, when they were kids, he and Isobelle had run down this very path. It was summer and the bush had been in full bloom. Isobelle stopped, awed and entranced by the small roses. Before he could stop her, she tried to pick one, but she'd tripped and fallen into the bush. Ridge had plucked her free and pulled the thorns from her skin. He'd even ripped up his old t-shirt to wrap around the places that were bleeding.

"Why would you do that?" he'd asked, wondering how she could have been so stupid. "You knew they had thorns."

Isobelle sniffed, wiping at the tears on her cheeks. "They're just so pretty, I thought they would make Daddy smile. He's been very sad since Mommy died."

Ridge remembered how, even then, he hated seeing her so sad.

He'd helped her to her feet, then pulled out his pocket knife, and searched for the biggest rose he could find. It took some time to reach it and by the time he'd cut it free he sported several cuts himself, but the smile she gave him was worth every scratch.

"Thank you," she said and stood on her toes to kiss him on the cheek before running off to give her dad the flower.

Now, as Ridge stared at what would most likely be that last batch of blooms before winter swept them away, he once again pulled out his pocket knife, searching among the blooms for the best one. Carefully, he cut it down.

Standing before her door, Ridge's jacket felt heavy, and he was definitely too warm for it despite the pleasant cooler weather. Heart racing, he waited for her to open the door, but no one came. He blew out a heavy breath. Of course no one was home. It fit his luck.

Carefully, he set the flower inside the cover of the book and laid it on the rocking chair by the front door.

Stuffing his hands into his pockets, Ridge backed away, both relieved and achingly disappointed.

"Hey."

Ridge looked up from the engine of an old jeep he was working on.

Chip, the owner of Chip's Auto Repair, was wiping his greasy hands on an already filthy rag. "We've been closed for almost an hour. You're not planning on starting on the van tonight, are you?"

Ridge wiped sweat from his forehead and looked back at the engine. "No. I just need to finish replacing the spark plugs on this then I'll be done. I'll start on the van first thing tomorrow."

Chip nodded. "Thanks, I always get so behind when you're off galavanting through the woods like Robin Hood or something." He laughed. "But what I was getting at is that you should go home."

Ridge shook his head, almost smiling. Chip was a couple years younger than him, friendly and mild-mannered. Everyone liked Chip. He'd been what people call a "miracle baby," surprising the Potts' who were in their mid-forties. Despite being a little spoiled, he was a good guy, and Ridge was grateful that he was willing to give him flexible hours and work around his hunting guide gig.

"But seriously," Chip said. "Don't stay late. In fact, just clean up and go home. You look exhausted."

Ridge eyed the engine. "I'm almost done. I'll lock up."

Chip sighed. "Fine. I'll see you tomorrow."

Ridge turned his focus back to his task. He didn't love being a mechanic, preferring to be outdoors, but he didn't mind it. It was satisfying to be able to actually fix something.

A few minutes later, he closed and locked the door to the auto shop. He climbed onto his motorcycle and sent his mom a text, letting her know he was on his way home in case she needed anything from the store before it closed. Just before he put on his helmet, a flash of yellow caught his eye.

Milton's stupid car flew past him. Ridge started his engine and followed for a while before easing to a stop.

Stargazer's Way was what their little town considered their "nightlife" spot. Lights were strung high overhead, crossing back and forth between little shops and cafes on each side of the one-way street. There was a piano on the sidewalk and a tiny fountain on the corner. It was the only place in the whole town that was open past nine pm and was their pride and joy.

Milton stepped out of his pointless car, buttoning his jacket as he hurried around to open the other side. Ridge was surprised the man would stoop to visiting this place.

Then his stomach twisted when Isobelle emerged from the vehicle, holding Milton's offered hand. Sour jealousy pulsed through him and he was about to peel away when his breath caught.

There, tucked under Isobelle's arm, was the book he'd left on her porch. She hugged it to her chest like it was the only thing keeping her from shattering.

But then she smiled at Milton and leaned into him as he stuck his arm around her shoulders.

Ridge revved his engine, gunning it to put as much distance between him and them as he could.

Just before he'd lost sight of them, Ridge thought he saw Isobelle look back over her shoulder in his direction.

* * *

Too fired up to go home, Ridge drove to Tuscal City to his favorite boxing gym. It had been a couple months since he'd been able to go. Fall always got busy, splitting his time between hunting trips and the auto shop.

He just needed a break, to get away from his mom, from the fire, from Milton's insufferable presence every-where he turned, and to try to forget the ache in his chest whenever he thought of Isobelle and the look on her face as she watched her shop burn to ashes.

The worst part was, there was absolutely nothing he could do about any of it. The tension was wound up so tight in his gut he felt more on edge than usual. He'd learned long ago not to trust people, to keep his head down and observe. It was amazing what you could learn, what people would unintentionally let slip when they didn't think you cared or were paying attention.

Ridge jerked open the gym door and was hit with familiar smells: sweat, blood, liniment, and just a hint of vinyl. Immediately, Ridge relaxed. This was safe.

He never told anyone he boxed, or that he was good at it, mostly because he worried it might remind Mom about how abusive Dad had been. He also wondered if Isobelle would think it was barbaric or if she would understand what this place meant to him. What it offered him. How it had saved him.

"Hey, stranger," a deep, throaty voice said, and immediately Ridge smiled. He turned to Victor, who already had his arms open wide. Ridge embraced the old man, his hair white against his black skin. "It's good to see you m'boy."

Pulling away, Ridge shook his head, still smiling. "You're looking younger every day, Vic."

The old man hooted, giving a gruff laugh. "Most people only wished they looked this good."

Victor was the only person, other than Isobelle, who could make Ridge laugh.

"How's your mom?" Vic asked, moving past him to pick up a stack of towels. Ridge intercepted and snatched them up, following the old man into the main room.

"She's... the same," he said, his gaze immediately going to the two men sparring in the ring that stood just off to the right. Several of the punching bags that lined the left wall were also occupied.

"Mmmmm," was all Victor offered in response. Ridge liked that about him, never pried into his personal business but he would listen, without judgment, whenever Ridge offered up more.

Weights clinked in the background as Ridge set the towels down on a shelf. "How are things here?"

Vic's eyes swept the room and Ridge could only imagine what he must see. This had been his home for over forty years. His wife and son had both passed away and he had no one. Guilt welled up inside of Ridge. He should have come to check on him sooner.

"Fine, fine." But now Vic turned his full gaze to Ridge, searching. Something in those dark eyes always seemed to cut right through Ridge's walls. "I have paperwork to finish up. Go punch something and work off some of that tension, then stop by my office on your way out." He clapped Ridge on the shoulder as he walked past.

Blowing out a deep breath, Ridge set down his gym bag and wrapped his hands, just as Vic had taught him almost ten years ago.

It was easy to call up his first memory of Vic. Ridge had just gotten his license and Mom had all but forced him from the house after Dad had wailed on him with both fists and belt, saying she needed a few things you could only get from the city's grocer. Back then he didn't stop to think if it was true; he'd just been grateful for the escape.

Ridge had kept his sunglasses on to cover his swollen eye but Vic had somehow just... known. Known that he needed someone, anyone. So there, in the chip aisle of the grocery store, he gave Ridge his card.

That was the night Dad pushed Mom down the stairs.

Ridge shook his head. He shouldn't have left her, and the guilt ate away at him every time she begged for more pain pills.

He threw a punch, imagining, wishing it was Dad's face.

An hour later, most of the gym was empty and Ridge was tired and drenched in sweat. His hands would be sore tomorrow but it was worth it. It was always worth it.

He cleaned up and made his way to Victor's office. The door was half open so Ridge went inside. He found the old man asleep in his chair.

Ridge silently moved up to the desk, debating on whether or not to wake him.

A stack of papers caught his eye. Brows furrowing, he carefully picked one up, and then another, and another. They were all about different cancer treatment options.

His gaze shot to Vic, still asleep in his chair. Cancer.

Ridge's chest hollowed out and he tried not to crumple the papers in his hand. Why hadn't Vic said anything? No, of course he wouldn't. Vic didn't share personal things very often but this was... this was... important! Life changing.

A raw ache built in Ridge's throat and he swallowed hard, drawing in a slow breath. Why was it only good things were destroyed? His mom, Isobelle's bookshop, and now Vic.

He replaced the papers and left the office, setting his gym bag by the door that he carefully closed behind him.

Ridge's body shook with a rage that surprised him. He stormed over to the closet and removed the cleaning supplies. Grabbing rags and disinfectant sprays, he tried to rein in his spiraling thoughts. Why couldn't he do something? Why was he so incapable of fixing anything? He couldn't cure cancer or magically come up with the money to fix Isobelle's shop. He couldn't heal Mom's knee or go back in time and defend her.

He scrubbed the mats with a viciousness born of too little for too long. Of self-loathing. Of regret. Ridge fell into the rhythm of it. Vic used to let him clean the gym as his way of paying for his use of it since he hadn't had any money.

Drops splattered on the mat beneath him, but whether it was sweat or tears, Ridge didn't know or care. After an hour of manic cleaning, the gym was done and Ridge threw down his rag, breathing hard.

"Feel better?" Vic's voice came from behind him.

Ridge didn't turn. "Not really."

Vic moved to stand beside him and together they stared at the empty room.

"I heard about the fire," Vic finally said, and Ridge dropped his head. "I'm sorry for your girl."

Ridge closed his eyes. He'd confided in Vic about his

36

feelings for Isobelle and the old man had called her his girl ever since. But she wasn't his; she never would be.

"Yeah," Ridge said. "Now would be a great time to be a millionaire."

Vic gave him a side glance. "Well, hell, if only that would actually solve our problems. But money don't solve the important ones."

"Maybe," Ridge agreed. "But it would sure make life a whole lot easier."

Vic chuckled. "Why don't you buy a poor old man a drink before you go."

Forty-five minutes later, Ridge was back on the road, heading home. Vic hadn't said a word about his cancer, so neither had he.

As he pulled onto the road that led to his house, he caught sight of red and blue lights flashing through the trees. Fear grabbed his heart in its cold, unforgiving hold when he found two police cars parked right in front of the porch.

Five

Ridge ran to the front door and threw it open. His mother sat at the kitchen table, tears spilling down her face while Sheriff Bronson sat beside her. Deputy Huskenson leaned against the counter, his face grim.

A sense of relief washed over him. For a moment, he thought they were here to tell him Mom had overdosed.

"Oh, Ridge," his mom said as she jumped to her feet. Flinging herself into his arms, she sobbed dramatically. "They think I stole meds and prescription pads. They say they caught me on a security camera this morning but I keep explaining it couldn't have been me. I was home with you!"

Ridge's blood went cold when she looked up at him, her face sunken, her eyes dull and desperate.

"Tell them, tell them it couldn't have been me," she said, gripping his shirt.

Swallowing hard, Ridge stared at her, his heart and mind at war. He should be the one taking care of her.

After all, it was his fault Dad had pushed her down the stairs, because she'd tried to protect him. Could he really let her go to prison?

She needed help, help he didn't know how to give her. She needed rehab, a therapist, something. Lying for her wouldn't do anything except send her to an early grave.

She pulled back, her face morphing from grief stricken to angry and desperate. Her eyes darkened. "Tell them the truth," she said slowly. "That I was with you."

Ridge looked over at the sheriff who had a patient, knowing look on his face, but it was the deputy who said, "The pharmacy installed a new camera behind the counter. Your mother was clearly caught taking a few pills while the pharmacist had her back turned."

"I'm telling you," his mom snapped, "you have the wrong person. I was with my son."

The sheriff and Ridge hadn't broken eye contact the whole time but Ridge gave the barest shake of his head.

"Come on, Marcie," the sheriff said. "Let's go down to the station."

She whirled on him. "Oh, so now you're ready to arrest me?" Her voice was high and hysterical. "Where were you when Jeff hit me or Ridge? Or when he broke my knee? You believed me then when I said I had just fallen, why won't you believe me now?"

"Mom," Ridge started, but she whirled and slapped him. He immediately reared back, not from pain–though is certainly stung–but from shock. She'd never hit him before. Ever.

Her hands flew to her mouth and for a long moment

they just... stared at each other. She didn't resist when the deputy put her in handcuffs.

"I—I'm sorry. Ridge, I'm so sorry."

He swallowed. Her agony was worse than her anger.

"Please don't let them take me." She was sobbing now. "Please!" She fought against the deputy as he dragged her out the door. "Don't let them take me! Help! Please help me!"

Ridge grabbed his arms and hugged his body. Why wasn't he doing anything? He should help her, lie, insist he was actually with her this morning. But the words were lodged in his throat. He couldn't save her by himself.

"You're doing the right thing, son," Sheriff Bronson said. "I've known your mother most of my life. That isn't her. She needs help."

At this, Ridge looked up. "And will she get it?"

"I swear on my life. I'll need some information from you and a statement, but after booking, if you want, we'll take her over to Tuscal City and get her evaluated at the hospital."

Ridge nodded.

Sheriff Bronson shifted. "It will cost—"

"Will it help?" Ridge's voice was gruff and his scowl felt deep, even to him.

"Maybe not at first, but give it time." The sheriff clapped him on the shoulder, just as Vic had, reminding Ridge that he was losing everyone he cared about.

When the police cars were finally gone and there was nothing left but deafening silence, Ridge stepped backward until his back hit the wall. Digging his hands into his hair, he slid to the floor.

Six

Ridge left another book on Isobelle's porch, not bothering to knock as he stuck a rose inside it, some of its petals falling between the pages. He'd been leaving them for a week now, the only highlight of his day as he dealt with paperwork, signing statements, and working with the police and doctors to help his mom.

"She finally admitted to taking prescription pads and a few pills here and there," the sheriff said. "Marcie never took enough to attract much notice so she's been getting away with it for years."

She still wouldn't speak to Ridge. Even if they were in the same room, she refused to look at him or even acknowledge his presence.

He sighed, starting up his motorcycle and driving into town. Everyone knew, of course. It was the way small towns were. It was hard to keep secrets and even harder to keep the stories accurate.

Already he'd heard several variations of what had

happened. Everything from his mom being an underground drug dealer to blackmailing people into looking the other way while she stole pain meds to get high for fun.

He parked his motorcycle in front of the grocery store and went inside. He kept his sunglasses on, as was his way, mostly to keep people from approaching him. It was amazing how that little trick seemed to deter people from starting a conversation.

But the whispers that followed him were like an itch he couldn't scratch. He had long become used to rumors. It had been especially bad in high school, just after he made the JV football team. He was filling out, lifting weights, and boxing. People were starting to notice and he had to admit, it felt good.

But then the troublesome trio—Charlotte and the Brambette twins, all blonde and beautiful, cornered him in the hallway. They'd wanted him to kiss each of them and determine which was the best kisser.

He'd been tempted, probably would have, if he was being honest. But just then, Isobelle appeared in the hallway, her nose stuck in a book. Then she'd looked up and saw them all standing there. The girls had draped themselves over him and he'd been enjoying it. Without saying hi like she usually did, she'd walked away without a word. He'd turned the girls down.

By the end of the day, the whole school knew what a "player" he was. The girls had decided to exact revenge by making up wild stories about him. It wasn't long before the tales had grown. How he slept around and convinced girls he loved them only to throw them away for the next pretty face.

At first, he'd tried to explain and tell everyone it wasn't true, but no one believed him. The girls were well off and popular, and he was just the... how had they put it? The dark, brooding boy who was all brawn and no brains.

After that, half the school treated him like he was the greatest thing to ever grace the halls, while the rest acted like he was pure poison.

The truth was, he got caught up in it all. He wasn't used to getting attention, not like that. By then, Dad had left and Ridge spent all of his free time working to provide for his crippled mom, who had sunken into a deep depression.

So the attention from the other students felt good, except for one thing. Isobelle was always there, watching him from across the room. Her mouth drawn into a tight line while boys made dirty jokes and crude comments. Every time he saw her his whole stomach would twist, dropping off a cliff of humiliation.

To this day, Ridge regretted not telling her the truth. She'd always remained polite and friendly, but distant, even to the point of avoiding him. Once they were out of high school and had become friends again, it felt stupid to even bring up.

Ridge grabbed a sandwich from the deli and a case of soda and headed to checkout. A few people stopped in their tracks, waiting for him to walk by as they cast wide-eyed glances at him.

He plunked his food onto the conveyor belt, wishing they had a self-checkout machine.

The teenage cashier stared at him for a few uncomfortable seconds then swallowed. "H-how are you today?"

Ridge pulled out his wallet, ignoring the question. She didn't really want to know and he really didn't want to answer.

"Right," she whispered, then added louder, "That will be eleven ninety-four."

Ridge handed her a twenty.

"Are you a drug dealer?" someone asked.

The cashier froze in the act of counting out his change and Ridge turned to face Mrs. Potts. She looked tense, worried, but her posture was straight and confident.

Of course she would be worried. He did work for her son, Chip, after all.

He removed his sunglasses and looked her in the eyes. She'd always been kind to him and he didn't want her to worry about him working in her son's shop.

"No."

She searched his face as if she could find the truth written in ink across his forehead.

"And your mother—"

"She's sick, Mrs. Potts. But she's getting help now. I hope her friends will stand by her despite all the false rumors so she doesn't feel alone or abandoned. Again."

He hadn't meant to say all that, but his protectiveness had reared up, angry at everyone who'd turned their back on them after his father was gone. He didn't know who had spread the rumor that Dad had left because his mom

45

had cheated, but if he ever found out he'd probably tear them to shreds.

To his surprise, she held his gaze, though her eyes looked a little glassy. Then, finally, she nodded. "Yes, of course. Of course. I will help in any way I can."

Ridge drew in a deep breath. He didn't say thank you. Even though she and his mom had once been friends, that had died when Dad left.

An unexpected surge of dark emotions reared up, clawing through his chest and into his throat, as though all his undealt with grief decided to suddenly appear. All he could think of was how everyone had turned away from them. The town hadn't helped. No one had even asked him if the rumors were true.

Swallowing hard, Ridge took the change from the wide-eyed girl, shoving it into his pocket, and snatching up his food. He practically ran through the doors, turning sharply and colliding into another body.

Seven

Ridge dropped the case of soda as he grabbed the person he'd collided with. There was a sharp cry.

He pulled back. "Oh, oh my gosh. Isobelle! I'm so sorry," he said, swooping to shove the sodas off her foot.

Her eyes were squeezed shut. "It's okay," she said, her voice breathy from pain. "I drop soda on my feet all the time."

"How bad is it?" Ridge gently held her ankle and removed her sandal, lifting her foot slightly to inspect the small gash on top.

Isobelle set a hand on his shoulder to steady herself and his heart jumped.

"It's nothing, promise."

He looked up at her face that was still scrunched, feeling completely wretched. "It's bleeding."

She puffed out a laugh. "Barely. It's just a flesh wound."

Ridge arched his brow. "Did you just quote Monty Python?"

She smiled, a tiny tear slipping down her cheek. Ridge's heart shriveled.

"Oh, come on," she said. "I'm hilarious."

He stood up, wishing she hadn't pulled her hand back. "I have a first aid kit in my saddlebags."

"I'm okay," Isobelle insisted and went to take a step, but she winced and started to crumple. Ridge immediately swooped her up into his arms, forcing her to throw her own around his neck, and started for his bike.

She gasped. "Wait!"

He stopped, fully expecting her to insist he put her down. After all, according to most of the town he was a player and now a drug dealer. Ridge's face was only inches from hers and he had to force down the heat building in his gut. He loved her brown eyes, always had. They were the most honest things he knew.

For a moment, Isobelle held his gaze, an odd look passing over her expression. His pulse jumped and his chest filled with more heat, spreading through his body. He'd never held her before, not like this. In his mind's eye he imagined her curling into his chest, pressing her body against his. Ridge wanted that. He wanted it so bad.

Someone cleared their throat as they passed by to enter the store. Isobelle's cheeks pinked. "Your sandwich."

Ridge blinked, his brain struggling to switch gears. "What?"

She pointed at the ground. "You dropped your sandwich too. It won't be any good if you leave it there."

He looked to where she pointed. Damn the sandwich. He shrugged. "It's fine. Let's look at your foot."

Isobelle laughed, her soft voice filling him with longing. Geez, what the crap was wrong with him?

"Just lean over so I can grab it."

Ridge almost ignored the suggestion, not caring about the stupid sandwich, but he did as she instructed, bending over so she could reach down and snatch up his lunch.

"Victory," she said, holding it up with one hand.

Ridge shook his head and walked to his bike, setting her gently on the seat.

"Go get your sodas," she said. He opened his mouth to protest but she added. "I'll wait here."

She grinned as he muttered under his breath, stalking back to pick up the case of soda he'd dropped on her foot.

By the time he made it back and put the case in one of the saddlebags, Isobelle had opened his sandwich and taken a bite.

He crossed his arms. "That's my lunch."

Isobelle picked out a piece of lettuce and put it in her mouth. "Mmm hmm."

"So that's the real reason you wanted to save my sandwich, because you were hungry."

Grinning at him, Isobelle said, "I admit to nothing." She took another large bite.

Ridge chuckled, loving every moment of this. "Let's fix up that foot."

Just then, a couple walked by, whispering, and Ridge caught the word "drugs."

Isobelle stilled. It was an instant reminder of the

rumors swirling about him and his mom. He crashed back to reality. He shouldn't be seen with Isobelle. He didn't want to drag her down with him.

Deciding it would be best to take her back to her car, he said, "You know—"

"Hey," Isobelle cut in, wrapping the sandwich back up. "Let's go to our spot at the park. It feels weird sitting here where everyone can gawk at my mangled foot."

"Mangled foot?" Ridge narrowed his eyes. "I thought it was only a flesh wound?"

"Yeah," she said, her eyes wide with exaggeration. "Exactly."

Ridge carefully climbed in front of Isobelle. When her arms slid around his waist, he had to draw in a slow, deep breath. Despite the cool temperature, he was sweating. She felt so good. It took everything in him not to drown in his craving for more of her.

He drove to the end of the brick wall that blocked off the park from one of the subdivisions. It tapered so the end was lower than the rest of the wall, and the trees blocked it from view. When they were in elementary school, he and Isobelle used to sit on the wall and watch the cool kids play. It was a crowd that didn't welcome or want a bookworm... or white trash.

Ridge parked his bike and pulled a couple sodas and his first aid kit from the saddlebags. He stuck a can in each coat pocket, making Isobelle smile, then he lifted her back into his arms and carried her to the wall.

His arms tightened around her, wishing he could keep her there, but he made himself set her gently down.

"Alright," he said, his voice a tad hoarse. "Let's look at this flesh wound."

She laughed as he took her cool foot in his warm hands.

"Why are you wearing sandals anyway? It's a little chilly."

Isobelle shrugged. "I was just going to get a few things to make for dinner tonight. I didn't think much of it."

Ridge gently poked and prodded, pushing her foot up and down, side to side to make sure nothing was fractured. "You're going to have a nasty bruise, but at least nothing's broken." There was a small gash across her skin, so Ridge opened his first aid kit.

Isobelle flinched when he applied some antibacterial ointment and wrapped it. He stood and sat beside her. "There. Hopefully that helps."

Isobelle ate another bite of his sandwich then passed it to him. Hiding a smile, Ridge also took a bite and handed it back. Her fingers brushed across his and heat traveled from his hand to his heart. They sat like that, eating in silence, passing the sandwich back and forth.

He wanted to ask her if she'd been getting all the books he'd left for her but he didn't want her to feel obligated to thank him. That's not why he was doing it. Ridge just hoped it helped her feel a little better.

Finally, he asked, "How are you holding up?" At the same time she said, "Can I ask you something?"

They both laughed.

"Please," Ridge said, "you first."

Isobelle drew in a slow breath.

He didn't like her hesitancy. It meant her question wouldn't be pleasant to answer.

"What really happened with your mom?"

Swallowing the food that was now like ash in his mouth, Ridge looked at the ground. Of course she would want to know. Actually, now that it was all in the open, he was glad she did. Everyone else seemed content to draw conclusions based on false information that held slivers of truth. At least she had the courage to talk to him.

"I'm sorry," Isobelle said. "It's none of my business—"

"No," Ridge cut in. "It's okay. I guess..." He dug the toe of his boot into the ground. "I guess it's hard to know where to start." So many painful memories came flooding back, memories he'd worked hard to burn and bury.

Isobelle sat quietly, waiting while he gathered his thoughts. She'd always been like that, never putting pressure on him to answer anything quickly. "Well, you know my dad wasn't a kind man—at least, not to my memory. He had a temper and...." Ridge's words trailed off. He didn't need to explain. She'd seen his bruises, even helped bandage him up a couple of times. He glanced at Isobelle but she just watched him, her eyes giving away nothing. At least there wasn't pity.

There was really no point in beating around the bush with this. He might as well just say it, like ripping the bandaid off. "The real reason he left was because he pushed my mom down the stairs. The fall broke her leg. My mom, of course, told everyone it was an accident." He huffed out a dark laugh. "It was *always* an accident. We'd been to the hospital enough times that the nurse refused to let my mom leave until she talked with the sheriff, and the doctor agreed.

"After that, my dad left, saying he'd come back when they were done fixing up Mom's knee but..." Ridge shook his head. "He never did. Never saw him again actually."

He rubbed his hands slowly back and forth, remembering how she'd cried and cried, begging the man to come back, calling out for him in her pain-riddled, drug-induced sleep. Ridge had only been sixteen years old, but sometimes, when her cries woke him in the middle of the night, he'd just stand in her doorway, watching her suck down more pain meds. Days turned into weeks, weeks turned into months, months to years.

He drew in a deep breath. "Between the pain and the depression, she got addicted to the meds. I didn't see it at first. I just thought she needed a lot of medication. By the time I realized what had happened..." He swallowed down the guilt that he'd unknowingly helped solidify her addiction.

Ridge couldn't bring himself to look at Isobelle now, to see the disgust in her eyes. He should have manned up long ago and done something, but it was never that simple. It was his fault Dad had pushed her.

"I tried to stop her once, well, twice actually," Ridge said. "The first time I just thought if I hid them she would eventually get over it but..." He rubbed his eyes. "She went crazy, suicidal. The second time, I was smarter. I'd done all the research I could on addiction, formed a plan, tried to do it smart but... I just couldn't be there all the time to watch her."

Isobelle still hadn't spoken a word so he finally looked

at her. Her brown eyes were glassy, as though she could feel a bit of his pain.

"That's..." she breathed. "I'm sorry." She placed a hand on his and emotion burned his throat. "You have to know it's not your fault. Not any of it."

He gripped her fingers. "Isobelle—"

An engine roar cut the air as a bright yellow car tore into the parking lot, skidding to a quick stop that made dust fly. Isobelle withdrew her hand and straightened.

Ridge's hackles rose as Milton opened his car door with a dazzling white smile.

"Darling!" he called, and sauntered toward them. "There you are. I've been looking for you everywhere."

Dark shades hid his freakishly bright blue eyes but Ridge thought he detected the slightest bit of annoyance coloring his tone.

"Oh," Isobelle said, glancing at Ridge, who took great care to remove any hint of emotion from his expression. "Sorry, I—"

Milton silenced her with a long kiss.

Ridge had to look away, grinding his teeth.

When Milton finally pulled back he was smiling again. "You said you were heading to the store so I thought I'd meet you there, but to my surprise, I'm told by the employees that they saw you ride off on a motorcycle."

Ridge didn't miss the way Milton pointedly ignored him.

"Oh, I..." Isobelle stammered. "Well, Ridge and I quite literally ran into each other and my foot got hurt—"

"What?" Milton immediately bent and inspected her foot. He tisked. "I told you you didn't need to worry about bringing anything over for dinner. We have cooks for that sort of thing." He laughed, making Ridge want to throat punch him again.

"Next time, listen to me, okay, darling?"

Isobelle pulled back, her expression tight. "Milton, while I appreciate you wanting to look out for me, I am a grown woman and *wanted* to make something. I can make my own decisions."

Milton pressed a hand to his heart, looking repentant, but Ridge thought he caught a tic in the guy's cheek.

"You're right, I'm sorry. I guess my protective nature gets in the way of good sense sometimes." He pulled a tiny pout and Ridge's sandwich almost came back up. He really couldn't stomach this anymore. Was Isobelle really attracted to this guy?

"Forgive me?" Milton pushed and Ridge cleared his throat, making them both turn to look at him.

"I am sorry again about dropping my soda and mutilating your foot, Izzy," he said. "I'll take you back to your car if you're ready."

"Oh, no need there, big fellow," Milton said cheerfully. "I got her." He swooped down and scooped up Isobelle. She squeaked and wrapped her arms around his neck.

Ridge's hand clamped tightly around the other man's arm before he could stop himself. "How about you let Isobelle decide?"

There was that tic in the cheek again, but Milton's voice was even. "Of course she can. I only meant she was coming over for dinner anyway so I might as well just take her."

It might have been his imagination, but Ridge could have sworn there was an odd inflection in Milton's voice when he said *take her.*

"It's okay, Ridge," Isobelle said, her voice soft, and Ridge had to mentally order his fingers to relax. "Milton's right. We are having dinner, so I can go with him."

Slowly, he nodded and stepped back, every inch of him crawling at the sight of Isobelle in his arms, especially while Milton's smile turned smug.

"Thank you for... this," Isobelle finished. Her words were weighted and Ridge knew what she meant; she was thanking him for sharing what he had. Still, it irked him that she was going with *him.*

"See ya around, big guy," Milton said, and strode to his stupid yellow car.

Something about him didn't feel right, and it was bothering Ridge. You couldn't see their spot from the road, he had checked before, and his bike was half hidden in the shade of the trees. Milton had torn in there, fast and sure, not like he was searching for anyone. How did he even find them?

Eight

R idge wiped sweat from his face as the salt stung his eyes. He paused to catch his breath for a moment before he swung at the punching bag again. He envisioned Milton's face as his fist connected over and over again.

Ridge had to leave in the morning on another guide trip. He didn't want to go now, not with his mom heading to rehab and Isobelle struggling with the aftermath of the fire, but this trip was short, just Friday through Sunday, and the wealthy Frenchman, Cogsworth, had offered to pay the price of a full week if Ridge would take him and a buddy out for a couple of days. He couldn't pass it up. Ever since his mom had been arrested, IOU's had been showing up from half the town. Apparently his mom had done a grand job at hiding just how deep her addiction went. He thought he'd been her only means of getting medication but apparently she'd begged money off of dozens of people. Just small amounts here and there that quickly added up over time.

She'd sworn to them it had been to pay bills and people felt sorry for her. Now, they all wanted their money back. The total was climbing quickly. Not to mention the bank was calling for payment on long overdue loans.

"You're getting sloppy." Vic's voice cut through his thoughts. "Straighten those feet, boy, you know better than that."

Ridge couldn't help it; a small smile tugged at his mouth and he straightened. "Maybe it's just your eyesight going bad, old man."

Vic scoffed, sweat glistening off his black skin. "You watch your mouth before I whoop yo' ass. Besides, I'm gonna live forever."

Ridge's smile faded, wondering just how long the old man had left.

Vic noticed. "What's on your mind, son? I haven't seen you this distracted in a while."

Shaking his head, Ridge grabbed his water bottle and drank deeply. When he finally came up for air, he had gathered enough strength to look Vic in the eyes.

"Mom got arrested for stealing prescription drugs."

Vic's expression didn't change, just gave a small nod, acknowledging that he knew how much it hurt Ridge.

"She hates me, too, because I wouldn't lie for her anymore. Because..." Ridge swallowed. "Because I told the judge I wanted rehab as part of her sentence."

Vic was silent and Ridge was grateful he didn't respond with pity or advice. Finally, the old man moved closer. "You did the right thing," he said, setting a hand on Ridge's shoulder.

Ridge said nothing, surprised by how much he

needed to hear that. Of course he knew it, logically, but his mother's anger and total disregard of him had hurt more than he wanted to admit.

"And your girl?" Vic asked. "How are things with her and the fire?"

Ridge huffed and unwrapped his hands. "She's not *my* girl."

"And who's fault is that?" Vic punched his arm. "You shoulda told her your feelings a long time ago."

Shaking his head, Ridge collected his stuff, throwing it out of the way to help Vic clean the gym. "She deserves better than me."

Vic snorted. "That's the stupidest thing I've ever heard you say and you've said a lot of stupid things." He grabbed the wide broom. "Why doesn't a good woman deserve a good man who loves her?"

"Oh, come on, Vic," Ridge said. "You know it's not that simple. I have nothing to offer her but debts passed down from a deadbeat dad, and a mom with an addiction. Besides," he continued, anger spilling into his words. "she has a prince now—a rich, polished prick with a stupid yellow car and teeth so white they'd blind you." He scrubbed viciously at an old stain on the mats. "She doesn't need me. She wouldn't want me."

Vic's hand grabbed his arm with surprising strength and hauled him to his feet. His dark eyes flashed in the gym lights.

"Enough with the self-pity crap." Vic was a whole head shorter than Ridge, but he shoved his face right up to his. "You think you're the only one with lousy circumstances? You think you're the only man life has ever ground to dust beneath its unfeeling boot?" He let go of Ridge. "History is full of men in situations far, far worse. Men who didn't quit just because everything about their life was shit."

Vic spun away and wiped a hand down his face. Shame filled Ridge. The old man was right, of course. From what little Ridge knew of the man's past, it had been nothing but heartache and pain. His wife and young son had been killed in a car accident, hit by a drunk driver. After that, Vic had sunk everything into the gym, almost losing it twice to bankruptcy before finally turning it into a place where the best of the best came to train.

"I'm sorry—"

"Don't be sorry," Vic snapped. "Be active. Stop wasting time and fight for what you want. Money isn't everything and if that girl doesn't know that then maybe she isn't who you need."

Silence settled between them, both men lost in their own thoughts.

Vic was right. He was always right. Ridge glanced at his watch—just after 11pm. It was too late to call Isobelle and he had to be up by 4am and would be out of cell reception before she was even awake. He would have to talk to her when he got back.

With the money from this trip he could start paying off debts and put money towards Mom's rehab. He would work extra at Chip's shop and start fixing up the house. He would talk to Isobelle and see if she would give him a chance.

Before he left the gym, Ridge shook Vic's hand. "Thanks."

The old man's dark eyes held so much depth, Ridge wondered what he was really thinking. "You deserve to be happy, son."

Ridge wasn't sure he deserved it, but he wanted it, with Isobelle.

A few hours later, Ridge silently stepped onto her porch and left another book from his collection, dark red petals placed between the pages. This book was called "Wait For Me," and he remembered the way she had talked about it, the way she'd said it made her cry and everyone should read it. So he had. It hadn't made him cry, but he understood why it would move someone to tears.

He prayed she would somehow understand what he was saying and wait for him before she made any decisions with Milton.

Just a few more days.

Nine

On his way home from the hunt, Ridge knew the moment he was back in cell reception because his phone lit up and buzzed with notifications. He pulled off onto the shoulder of the road and ran through every message. He had several from his mom's attorney and the rehab facility. Several texts from Chip, some missed calls, emails from potential clients asking for more information about hunting trips, and one text from Isobelle.

Heart pounding faster than it had all weekend despite all the hiking they'd done, Ridge opened it. It had been sent the morning he'd left.

"Thanks again for sharing your sandwich with me and for telling me about your mom. If you have time, maybe I could talk with you again. I have some things I'm trying to figure out and could use some help sorting my thoughts."

Ridge reread it three more times. It wasn't quite the message he'd expected, but it was something. He had so much to tell her. Ridge started to type a return message when the reception dropped again. With a huff of frustration, he threw the truck into drive and started back down the road. He came around a bend, remembering it was where he first spotted Milton's yellow sports car. His lip curled.

He waited until he pulled up to his house before he texted Isobelle back, explaining where he'd been and that he just got home but was heading into town in a few minutes and could meet with her there or at her house.

Anticipation made his stomach twist and flip as he raced through a shower and a shave. Then, he threw on his best jeans, no holes this time, and a black henley. Supposedly girls liked henleys on men—at least that's what Charlotte had always told him.

Isobelle still hadn't messaged him back but he headed toward town anyway, hoping to hear from her any moment. He was just passing the gas station when his phone buzzed. A smile broke out across his face and he tapped the text notification.

"I hope you had a good trip. It's okay. It doesn't matter anymore. You should get some rest."

His smile quickly dropped into a deep frown. What did that mean? Worry slithered through him, leaking into all his thoughts like poison. Something wasn't right. He sent back a voice text.

"Where are you?"

He waited but there was no reply. A weight settled in his gut. Ridge drove up and down the streets, checking every place he could think of. Nothing. He finally tried calling Isobelle, something he'd never actually done in all the years they'd known each other, but it went unanswered.

A cold sweat built on Ridge's skin as he strangled his truck's steering wheel. Finally, he spotted a flash of blue as he drove by the school. There she was, sitting on a swing in the empty playground.

Ridge parked and opened his door, never taking his eyes from her. Her gaze was fixed on the place across from the school where her bookstore had once been, where now there was only black rubble and the landscape beyond.

The closer he got the more his gut twisted. Her expression was so utterly... forlorn. She didn't even look up when his boots crunched on the wood chips that covered the ground beneath the swings.

"Izzy?" He said her name softly but she still just... stared ahead. He sat in the swing next to her, not saying anything else. A single tear trickled down her cheek and Ridge had to grip the chains to keep from wiping it away.

Finally, Isobelle sniffed. "When I was in kindergarten the teacher told us to draw a picture of what we wanted to be when we grew up." She swiped at her face. "I drew a picture of myself on a unicorn holding a book." She smiled and glanced at him. "I just knew that I would be the first person to ever find a real unicorn and we would live in a castle full of books where food magically appeared and the dishes talked. My dad kept that drawing on the fridge for a very long time. So long that I still remember almost every detail of it."

Ridge remained silent. His mom often talked about odd things when she was feeling down. He used to try to make it better, always feeling like it was his fault that she had crumbled. But then, one day, she snapped at him, telling him to stop making it worse by always trying to fix things. It just made her feel guilty that he made it all about him. She just needed someone to listen, someone to just... *be* there, so she wasn't alone.

Over the years Ridge had had to learn to do just that —listen. It wasn't easy when everything in him wanted to jump up and fix it all somehow, but some things couldn't be handled that way. So, he waited.

Isobelle gave a small laugh. "I never did find that unicorn, but I thought maybe I'd managed to get that castle full of books." She drew in a deep breath. "It's okay to let some dreams go. Dad is what's most important right now."

Her phone rang, and when she looked at the number she apologized, saying she had to take it. That's when Ridge noticed a book peeking out from the top of her purse—the book he'd left for her before his trip. He smiled, burning up with all the words he had to say.

"Are you sure?" Isobelle's surprised voice brought him back to focus. "No, that's impossible. We've never brought any into the shop. Yes, I'm positive."

There was a long silence while she listened and Ridge fidgeted, a growing sense of dread filling him.

"Yes, alright. Thank you for the information." Pause. "Yes, please let me know. Thanks. Bye." She hung up and stared at the phone in her hand like she's never seen one before.

"Isobelle? What is it?" he asked.

"That was the fire marshall." She finally looked at him. "They determined the cause of the fire."

Ridge straightened in the swing. "What was it?"

She shook her head. "They said there were two propane tanks in the basement that had exploded. But—" Isobelle still stared at the phone.

"But what?" he prodded.

She lifted her eyes to his. "I've never purchased propane tanks. And... Dad wouldn't have done it. He never goes into the basement. It's too hard on his knees."

A wash of ice slid over Ridge. "Are you saying they think the fire was deliberate?"

Isobelle scrunched up her face. "That's what it sounds like but... why would anyone want to burn down a bookstore? Unless..." Her eyes went wide. "Unless it was a crazed fan or stalker of Gabrielle's? Maybe they didn't want her coming here? I mean, she's an international bestseller with a massive fanbase. Or—" She looked around. "Do you think there's someone here who didn't want her coming? Because then it would attract more people to our town?"

Ridge shook his head. Those both seemed pretty far fetched... but not necessarily impossible. "I don't know," he said, trying to work through his own thoughts. There was something there, something hovering at the edges of his memory, like he'd just woken from a dream, and the harder he tried to remember it, the more it slipped away.

The roar of an engine and a flash of yellow made them both look up. Milton's car sped into the school parking lot, pulling to a stop right in front of the playground.

Ridge frowned, the hairs on his neck rising.

Milton stepped from the car, all white teeth and perfect hair, as usual. "There you are, babe! I've been trying to call but you haven't been answering." He sauntered toward them and Ridge felt his frown deepen. In all the time he'd been here, Isobelle had only received one phone call.

Milton looked between them. "Is everything okay? Isobelle, is this guy bothering you? Cause honestly, you always look upset when he's around."

Ridge stood up slowly, anger rising in his gut.

Isobelle stood too. "Oh, no, it's not like that at all. I—"

"It might not be a good idea being seen with him, anyway," Milton cut in. "Now that we're together, you'll be the center of attention and—"

"Together?" The word spilled from Ridge before he could choke it back down.

Milton grinned and pulled Isobelle to him. "That's right. This beautiful girl is now all mine."

Isobelle's brow furrowed and she tucked her hair behind her ear, looking back and forth between the two of them. "Can I talk with Ridge for just a moment? Then we'll go."

Milton's smile was so tight, Ridge thought he might split a lip.

"Please, Milton. It'll only be a moment."

"Of course," he finally said. "I'll be by the car." He kissed her, hard, and Ridge had to look away. He tried not to pace but he was so... so agitated he couldn't help it.

The second Milton was out of earshot, Ridge

rounded on Isobelle. "Are you serious? You're dating him? Why?"

He knew it wasn't any of his business, and of course, he knew why she'd choose him. Milton was everything Ridge wasn't.

Isobelle pulled the book from her purse and caressed the cover. "Milton's been pursuing me for a long time now. At least six months."

This made Ridge step back. "What?"

"It started with an email here and there, then texts, phone calls, and video chats. He'd offer to fly me places and take me to fancy restaurants. None of that matters to me, of course, but he's been very persistent." She glanced at Ridge. No doubt his scowl was fierce, but he couldn't help it.

"Since the fire, Milton has been very sweet. Helping to take care of me and Dad, helping with the investigation, offering to chat with the insurance company. He's been great. A little clingy, but I think that's just because he's worried about me."

Isobelle bit her lip. "But when he started leaving these books for me, I realized that maybe I was looking at him all the wrong ways. He knew what all my favorites were."

Ridge opened his mouth, then closed it again, stunned. Milton had taken credit for the books. *His* books.

He found his voice. "Isobelle, listen. You can't date him. Milton is a liar. He's not who he claims to be and quite frankly, I'm surprised you let him control you so much."

Isobelle's head snapped up, and for the first time in a

very long while, there was real fire in her eyes. "He doesn't control me. He's worried, that's all. And how dare you call him a liar. He's been helping me with so many things, even Dad. He's gone to the hospital every day to check on him."

She gripped the paperback so tight her fingers were white. "These books have been everything, *everything* for me. Maybe you can't understand, maybe its stupid to you, but his thoughtfulness is what's getting me through all of this." Her eyes shone with tears. "So don't you dare tell me what to do. We're not in high school anymore. I'm not like the other girls, Ridge. I'm not yours. I never have been."

Her angry words killed his confession about the books before it left his mouth, sucking the air from his lungs. Something in him splintered. There it was. Finally, the truth. She didn't want him.

Of course she wouldn't want him, why would she? He was nothing. She saw him as such and he shouldn't have hoped otherwise.

Ridge straightened burying the hurt deep. She still needed to know the truth about Milton.

"Isobelle, just—"

"No!" She backed away. "Enough. Just leave me alone." She spun and ran to Milton, who held the car door open for her. As soon as it was closed, Milton sauntered over to Ridge and for the first time, his mask seemed to melt away. His eyes held a dark glint that made Ridge's stomach curl.

"I think it's time you left Isobelle alone," Milton said. "It's clear she wants nothing to do with you."

Ridge seethed. "You're a lying bastard. You won Isobelle over with a lie."

Milton shrugged. "I was close anyway. This just tipped the scales in my favor faster. I never lose, not with money or women and certainly not to the likes of you." He glanced back at his car. "I figured the books were from you and right now, Isobelle doesn't need lowlife bottom feeders with druggie moms pulling her down even further. I was doing her a favor."

Ridge's fist flew so hard and fast he barely registered the impact when it connected with Milton's face.

It was enough to send him to the ground. Isobelle opened the car door, screaming at him to stop. Milton looked up, his eyes black with rage so raw, Ridge lifted his fists instinctively. Milton smiled, wiping the blood from his lip. "She'll never believe anything you say now."

Then Isobelle was there, dropping down beside the snake, taking his face between her hands.

Ridge unclenched his fists. "Isobelle—"

"Stop!" Her eyes were red, her cheeks wet as she helped Milton up. "I don't know what's wrong with you but just leave us alone."

For a moment, Ridge couldn't move. It had all happened so fast. Too fast. Everything was wrong.

Milton insisted she get in the car first, and as he walked toward the driver's side, he mouthed the words so clearly Ridge didn't need to hear them to know them.

"I win."

Ridge burst into an all-out run, yelling Isobelle's name, but the car sped away before he was close enough to touch it.

Ten

Ridge drove to Chip's shop, not wanting to go home. Was he overreacting because Isobelle had chosen Milton? No, if the man was willing to lie about something as simple as a few books, what else was he lying about? And again, how had he known they were at the park? A dark foreboding filled him and he slammed the steering wheel, appreciating the pain that radiated up his arm.

He looked around the empty parking lot, only just now remembering that it was Sunday and the mechanics shop was closed. Ridge dragged a hand down his face, his thoughts in chaos. A chime went off on his phone, a reminder that he needed to call Mom's lawyer. With a sigh, he called his mom instead.

The receptionist at the rehab facility put him on hold while she went to find Mom. Ridge traced a finger over his steering wheel, silently praying she would finally be willing to talk to him. He just needed something to finally be okay in his life.

Ridge's head drooped when the receptionist said Mom was unavailable. What she really meant was, Mom didn't want to speak with him. So, he left a message, not that it mattered. She never called him back.

A knock on his window startled him and he turned to find Chip standing there. Ridge rolled down his window.

Chip gave him a strange look. "Are you okay?"

No. he wasn't, but Ridge wasn't used to having friends or talking or opening up to anyone about anything. Vic and Isobelle had been the only people he'd ever done that with. No one else felt safe enough but right now, he was going crazy.

"No," he finally admitted but couldn't get any more words out.

Chip was silent for a moment then said, "Come inside."

Ridge followed him through the door, the scent of metal and gas and oil slamming into him, old and familiar.

Once Chip flipped on a light, barely illuminating a part of the small shop, he waved Ridge to the office. "Want a drink?"

"No, thanks."

Chip nodded and grabbed a bottle of water. He sat in the chair behind a desk cluttered with papers and tools. "What's going on?"

Ridge sank into a chair opposite the desk and frowned. Where did he even begin, and was Chip even a good person to talk to about this? He cleared his throat. "What do you know of Milton Freewater?"

Chip's worried expression immediately turned wary and he straightened, searching Ridge's face.

This made Ridge lean forward. "What?"

"Why do you ask?" Chip's voice was... cautious.

Ridge was too wound up for games or tiptoeing around anything anymore. "There's something off with him. I don't trust him and I don't trust his interest in Isobelle." There, he'd said it.

Chip nodded, looking at the drink in his hands. "I don't have a lot of experience with him. Rich guys like that usually go over to Tuscal City to get their fancy cars worked on. But a few weeks back, his sports car got towed in here because of a flat." He shook his head. "He didn't even know he had to have a key for the lugnuts on his tires. He wasn't happy about being here. The guy gave off a bit of a slimy vibe, if you know what I mean, but he paid fair and square. Don't ask me why a richy like that would have a couple of propane tanks in his back seat. I'm surprised he even knew what they were." Chip guzzled his water.

The air in Ridge's lungs burned cold. "What did you say?"

Chip looked a little confused. "Which part?"

"You said he had propane tanks in his back seat." Ridge thought back to his first encounter with Milton. He had seen them too.

"Yeah. We had to take them out to search for the key—"

"Is there anything else you can remember? Did anything happen or did you find anything else in the car?"

73

Chip gave him an odd look. "Are you in some kind of trouble? Something with your mom?"

"No." Ridge leaned against the desk. "No, I'm fine, but I think Isobelle might be in trouble."

"Isobelle?"

"Please, Chip," Ridge ground out through clenched teeth. "It's important."

Chip scratched his cheek. "Sorry, Ridge. He was on his phone most of the time, arguing with someone. All I heard him say was that he had everything under control and things would be able to move forward in a couple weeks. Probably something to do with them buying up all the land along the waterfront."

This made Ridge sit bolt straight. "What?"

Chip glanced to the side, then down at his water bottle. "I'm not really supposed to know about it, but Charlie Pascus came in with a new truck. Wanted me to look over a few things and probably show it off. When I asked how he'd managed to get it, he told me someone had just paid double what his property was worth. Said he couldn't tell me who, but then later mentioned offhand that he was curious what the Freewaters wanted to do with it."

Ridge stood. "It was him." He dug his hand into his hair. "It has to be. It all makes sense!"

Chip stood too, looking wary. "You better explain."

"It's why he had the tanks and why he's trying to convince Isobelle to sell the property to him. He wants the land! But why?"

"Ridge, you're making no sense."

Ridge's mind raced. "Thanks, Chip. I need to go." He left, not caring that Chip's mouth literally hung open. Pulling his cell from his pocket, he found the name he was looking for and dialed.

"Hey, it's Ridge. I need to see you. Right now."

Eleven

By Monday night, after hours of phone calls, house calls, and trips between Tuscal and Bear River, Ridge had collected enough evidence to convince him that Milton was guilty. Probably not enough to get an outright conviction, but enough it might sway a jury.

The sheriff warned Ridge to stay away from Milton and Isobelle and let the proper authorities handle it, but waiting around for a warrant was asking too much.

He killed the engine to his motorcycle and ran up the steps to Isobelle's house. After knocking and ringing several times with no response, he went around the home, peering through windows and even knocking on the back door, but no one was home.

He spun, searching the grounds, calling Isobelle's name, but there was only silence. He tried Isobelle's cell phone for the hundredth time—straight to voicemail. He'd already left half a dozen messages and texts but she hasn't responded to any of them.

A gnawing dread ate at his gut. Something was wrong. No, everything was wrong, he could feel it. Ridge drove all over town, checking all the places he thought she might go, even stopping to ask several people if they'd seen her, but no one had.

He dialed the sheriff's number.

"What is it, Ridge?" Sheriff Bronson sounded both annoyed and tired.

"I can't find Isobelle anywhere. No one knows where she is."

There was a long sigh on the other end. "Leave it alone, Ridge. I'm serious. The warrant should be coming in at any time now. I'm sure she's fine. Just don't do anything stu—"

Ridge hung up and turned his bike toward the Freewater mansion just as the sun slipped below the horizon.

Ridge had never been so tempted to pull an unrealistic movie stunt as he was when the mansion gates came into view. If only ramming through them was actually a thing.

Lights and cameras lined the front of the gates and an armed security guard sat in a small booth right outside the door. "Oh, please," Ridge muttered. This place was so out of the way hardly anyone had actually seen it. He certainly never had.

He came to a stop beside the booth. Ridge's eyebrows lifted. "Bradley? I didn't know you worked here."

Bradley grinned. "Hey, Ridge. Yeah, it's only my third shift. I work a couple evenings a week. It's pretty simple.

Mostly I just play games on my phone." Then he glanced around as though he probably shouldn't admit that out loud.

"Well, good for you." Ridge smiled, trying to appear calm though his pulse raced with a frantic urgency. "Hey, I need to speak with Milton."

Bradley grabbed a clipboard and squinted at it. "Do you have an appointment?"

"No, it's kind of a last minute thing and I don't have his number."

The young security guard shifted, suddenly uncomfortable. "I'm not really supposed to let anyone in without an appointment, but I can buzz back and see if Mr. Freewater will see you."

Ridge spread his fingers. "Come on, Brad. You've known me your whole life. Remember when you got in trouble with—"

"Okay, okay," Bradley cut in, holding up his hands as if he didn't want Ridge to mention the night he'd gotten drunk and accidentally driven his car into the river. Ridge had been coming home from a hunting trip and helped tow him out and clean up the car.

"I'll let you in," he grumbled. "But I'll still need to buzz back and let Mr. Freewater know you're coming." He shook his head. "I better not get fired for this."

Bradley pushed a button and the gates slid open.

"Thanks," Ridge said, and eased his bike forward

Even though the mansion had been here since his grandfather's time, Ridge had only ever driven by the grounds a couple of times and had never actually seen the house. People in the Freewater's circle didn't typically condescend down to his level. Another reason why Milton's interest in Isobelle seemed odd, unless she really was just a challenge to conquer for him.

He eased down a long driveway lined with thick trees, a heavy feeling of dread pressing down on him. It was all so eerie in the dark.

Finally, the trees dropped away to reveal what was really more of a castle. Towering turrets and spires looked down their noses on him. The bright lights from the mansion shone out over what looked like a vast garden of rose bushes, but it was hard to know for sure in the fading light.

He killed the engine and climbed the steps to the excessively tall doors. The doorbell made no sound that he could hear when he pushed it, but a few moments later, the door opened to reveal a tall, thin man.

Ridge shook his head. They had a butler. Of course there would be a butler.

The man glanced over Ridge, then beyond him to his bike with an eye of disdain. "May I help you?" The arrogant disgust was thick in his tone.

Ridge shoved his hands into his pockets, surprised they were shaking. "I'm here to see Milt—Mr. Freewater."

The butler was quiet for a long time, then said, "I'll see if he has time to meet with you." The door slammed shut. Ridge stood there for a long moment. There was no way Milton was going to agree to see him.

He grabbed the handle and pushed open the door. No one was there to stop him. He closed it quietly behind him and scrunched his face. Did someone really need that much space between the floor and the ceiling?

Ridge moved into the foyer, unsure of where to go. A wide, sweeping staircase led to an upstairs balcony. Long hallways stretched out on both the right and the left of the room and a vast living room opened up on the left. Everything seemed... white. White carpets spread out in all directions. The walls were white, the curtains were white, even the vases holding white flowers were white. At least some of the furniture was a pale gray.

"No imagination," Ridge muttered and started to move down a hallway.

A young woman came out of a room and screeched when she saw him, almost dropping her armful of white sheets.

"Sorry," they both said at the same time. She looked at him with wide eyes, clearly not used to seeing someone just walking around the massive place.

"Sorry," Ridge said again. "I'm supposed to be meeting with Milton but I'm not quite sure where to go."

Her mouth dangled open and Ridge knew he recognized her from town but couldn't think of her name.

"Would you mind pointing me in the direction of his office?" Ridge tried.

She pointed up. "Up the stairs to the right, down the hall to the right again. It's at the end," she finally squeaked out.

Ridge tried to smile at her. "Thank you." He hurried to follow her directions, taking the stairs two at a time, his gut churning with unease.

At the end of the hall, the butler was closing a door

behind him, and Ridge ducked into a darkened doorway, pressing into the shadows.

With his nose still in the air, the man swept right by him, not looking anywhere but straight ahead.

As soon as he was moving down the stairs, Ridge sprinted for the door. It opened without a sound. Clearly, squeaky hinges were beneath the Freewaters.

Milton was standing with his back to the door, shuffling through some papers on a long and dark, very ornate desk. At least it wasn't white.

Ridge let the door click behind him.

"That was fast," Milton said without looking up. "Did you manage to take out the trash already?" Milton chuckled then finally looked up. The smile on his face faded and something Ridge couldn't quite put his finger on filled his expression. Dread, maybe?

"You wouldn't be talking about me, would you?" Ridge said as he smiled.

Milton straightened, his own bright smile returning to his face. "Don't be silly, I just sent my butler to retrieve you. I believe you wanted to speak with me. Come in, sit."

"I'd rather stand," Ridge said, moving further into the room.

Milton shrugged, leaning back against the desk. "Suit yourself. What did you need to see me about so urgently?"

Ridge looked around the study, making a show of inspecting the many trophies, medals, and certificates that were displayed for fencing, wrestling, and marksmanship. Photo after photo of Milton smiling with someone important—-or worse, just Milton himself—were displayed everywhere. Ridge tried not to sneer. Oddly enough, there was only one small photo of Milton and his dad. It was from a fishing trip, a large boat behind them. Milton held up a fish while his father smiled proudly beside him. Typical.

Books and souvenirs from all over the world were displayed on bookshelves. Everything about the room spoke of wealth and privilege.

Ridge shook his head. "You have all this, but it's not enough. You still want more."

Milton tilted his head, watching him silently. Waiting. Confident. Smug.

"What I can't figure out is the why." Ridge shook a finger like he was trying to mentally piece together a puzzle.

Sighing, Milton looked positively bored. "Could you try to make sense?"

"I know it was you," Ridge said. "You started the fire in the bookstore."

Milton laughed. "More of your outlandish claims? First you try to convince Isobelle that I'm a liar and now this." He shook his head. "When are you going to learn that they only make you look even more pathetic than you already are? No matter what you conjure up about me, Isobelle will never be yours." His eyes flashed.

Ridge shook his head. "Isobelle isn't an item to be won or lost." He laughed, though his heart hurt. "She will never love me, not like that. That's not what this is about. Isobelle deserves to know what sort of slimeball she's mixed up with."

He moved even closer. "I saw the propane tanks in your car that day on the road when you had a flat tire. Chip will testify that he had to remove two propane tanks from your backseat when he was searching for the key to the lugnuts on your tires."

Ridge felt a flicker of satisfaction when Milton's smug expression faltered.

"The cashier at the hardware store on the outskirts of Tuscal, where you paid cash, remembers you. Hard to forget that ugly yellow tin can you drive around."

Milton scoffed. "Oh please, since when was owning your own grill and replacing the tanks a crime?" He leaned forward, his eyes glinting. "I get that you probably don't understand this, but having enough money to pay cash for things doesn't make you a criminal."

There was a knock on the door and the butler opened it. "Forgive me sir, but—" He cut off when he saw Ridge. "Shall I call security?"

Milton held up a hand. "It's quite alright, Bexley." His eyes roved over Ridge and there was a definite sneer when he said, "Ridge here was simply entertaining me with the most outrageous jokes." He glanced at the butler. "Be sure to close the door on your way out."

Bexley seemed annoyed he was being dismissed, but after a moment he inclined his head. "Yes, sir."

"Forgive the interruption," Milton said once the door was closed. He waved a hand. "Do go on."

Ridge stared at the closed door. "Ridiculous. Does he wipe for you too? Tuck you in at night?"

Milton's lips thinned.

"Well," Ridge said, leisurely examining the items

along the wall again. "You're right. I don't know much about grilling or endless amounts of cash, but I did learn something interesting about fire recently. Did you know that they can pull fingerprints from burnt metal?" He glanced at Milton, whose expression gave nothing away. "I mean, there's lots of factors involved, but even wiping down something like, say... a couple of propane tanks used to intentionally start a fire, might not be enough to get rid of evidence." He faced Milton full-on. "It's only a matter of time before the sheriff arrives with your arrest warrant."

Silence hovered between them for a long moment. A tiny crease formed between Milton's brow before it smoothed.

"My my, who would have thought that the scrawny kid from the wrong side of town would have grown up to have such a grand and... disturbed imagination." Milton leaned back against the front of the desk, his hand gripping the edge on either side of him. "First, you accuse me of lying, and now you're here with wild accusations of me blowing up my girlfriend's dream." He shook his head, his face a mask of pity. "Perhaps your father beat you one too many times, or maybe it was your mother's drugs that messed up your brain."

A hot rage flared inside Ridge and his hands curled into fists. It took everything in him to keep his voice even. "I know you've purchased all the land along the lakefront. There was only one key piece left, right in the middle. A piece of property that belonged to an old man and his daughter. An old man who refused to sell to you."

Milton's eyes were blue steel.

"So you decided to go about things another way to try and force Isobelle's hand."

"Not force, convince." Milton shrugged. "Either way, it's your word against mine."

There was a small click and Ridge saw a hidden compartment pop open right next to Milton. From the drawer, he pulled a gun.

Twelve

Ridge's blood went cold. The man was truly crazy.

"Or, maybe," Milton said, his voice taking on an unnervingly calm edge. "It was you who burned down the bookstore out of jealousy then came to me and begged for money so you could disappear. When I refused, the guilt about what you'd done, coupled with your mom's addiction and arrest, was too much so you took your own life."

No, not crazy. Insane. Milton was insane. Ridge let out a harsh laugh. "You're going to kill me? Seriously? You think that will work?"

Milton's eyes darkened. "Isobelle is mine, the property will be mine, you'll be dead, and I'll have an army of lawyers at my back." He cocked his head. "I'll have everything."

There was a small sniff and they both turned toward the second entrance at the side of the room. Isobelle stood there with wide eyes, her face pale. Milton hid the gun from her view.

"Is it true?" she asked, her voice soft but hard. "Is what Ridge said true?"

Milton took a step forward but her expression warned him not to come any closer and he stopped. "Please, darling. Don't listen to him. Don't let his lies come between—"

"What was the name of the first book you gave me?"

This pulled Milton up short. "What?"

"The books you left me, the ones you said you knew were my favorite, what was the name of the first one you left me?"

Milton's voice was soft and pleading. "None of that matters. I love you. I've only wanted to help. Am I not paying for your father's medical bills? Have I not gone to see him every day? Have I not been right by your side, encouraging you to do the right thing?"

Isobelle's expression had faltered, but at the last remark, her eyes glinted. Slowly, she held up a sheet of paper. "This sales contract I just signed?" Deliberately, she gripped the document with both and ripped it in half.

"No!" Milton yelled, and started forward.

"It has never been the right thing to sell," Isobelle snapped, ripping it over and over again.

Milton's face solidified into a cold fury.

Ridge lunged, his shoulder slamming into the other man's chest.

Landing hard on the desk, the two men grappled for the gun. Ridge threw a punch as Milton twisted out from under his hold, throwing an elbow. The impact sent stars across Ridge's vision. Milton was far stronger than Ridge had given him credit for and doubt bled into his mind. He couldn't save his mom. He couldn't protect Isobelle.

Milton raised a fist but then toppled, falling hard next to Ridge. Isobelle sucked in deep breaths, her arms outstretched from shoving Milton down. Ridge rolled to his knees, pinning Milton on his back. Grabbing his arm, Ridge pounded the guy's wrist into the edge of the desk over and over until there was a cracking noise. Milton screamed, releasing the gun. It clattered to the floor where Isobelle grabbed it and backed away toward the wall.

Ridge stood, backing away too, feeling blood trickle from a cut by his eye.

Milton groaned and rolled over, his back toward them.

"Izzy, we need to call the police—"

Milton wheezed out a laugh.

Ridge and Isobelle shared a glance as he staggered to his feet, still laughing.

"How tragic," Milton said. "Ridge, a man so pathetic and desperate, he breaks into my house and assaults me in an attempt to steal back Isobelle, who refuses to go with him. Driven mad with jealousy, Ridge shoots her then turns the gun on himself."

Milton turned around, his face already beginning to swell. His blue eyes were bright and half crazed. He grinned, showing a row of bloody teeth.

"The only good thing that came out of any of this is that Isobelle and her father signed over the land to me before she died. No one will remember her when casinos and resorts and strip clubs line the waterfront."

"He's mad," Isobelle whispered. She pulled her phone from her back pocket and dialed 9-1-1.

Milton's face fell. "We could have been happy together," he said, wiping blood from his cheek. "We made a beautiful couple." His face hardened. "I would have given you everything. Everything!"

Ridge took the gun from Isobelle's trembling hands as she spoke with the operator. "Let's go."

Milton shook his head. "Oh, I don't think so." There was a sharp click and another hidden compartment popped open. Milton reached into the drawer, grabbing something, then raised his arm. Instinctively, Ridge shoved Isobelle to the side.

A pop.

There was a sharp pain in his side as Ridge raised the gun and fired back. The sound seemed muted, but Milton toppled. Ridge lowered his arm, the smell of gunpowder dissipating into the air. His ears rang. Someone called his name but his mind felt muddled as he stared at Milton's body.

Isobelle was there, her mouth moving. He blinked, struggling to focus on her words.

"You've been shot."

Her frantic words finally made sense.

"Lay down."

Ridge stared into her wide, terrified eyes. She'd looked at him like that before. She'd only been seven years old when he'd fallen out of a tree, knocking the air from his lungs. She'd thought he was dying. He discovered he liked it when she was worried about him.

"Lay down," Isobelle said again, pulling on his arm. Ridge's leg caved and he went down hard.

Pain, like hot knives dug into him and he cried out.

Isobelle hovered over him, then she threw open his jacket. He looked down. There was a small hole in his dark green t-shirt. "Crap," he panted. "I liked this shirt."

The door burst open and the butler charged in, his eyes going wide at the scene. "Master Milton!" He ran to the body.

"You killed him!" Bexley screeched, staring at Milton laying crumpled on the floor. He spun, his face contorted in rage. He grabbed an envelope knife off the desk and stalked toward them, but Isobelle was on her feet in an instant, holding the gun Ridge had dropped with a steady hand.

The man froze.

"I've already called the police," she said. "They'll be here any moment. In the meantime, I suggest you keep away from us or you'll be joining him." She waved the gun at Milton.

Bexley dropped the knife, his hands raised as he slowly backed from the room.

Isobelle dropped back down beside Ridge.

"That was hot," he said, trying not to breathe hard. It hurt too much.

Isobelle didn't look away from her task. "You forget I took first place in the Fall Festival Shooting contest."

He tried to grin. "I didn't forget."

She froze, staring at the floor beside him as blood pooled and spread. "I think the bullet went all the way through," she whispered, then, without another word, tore his shirt open and tipped him to the side.

Ridge gritted his teeth against the pain.

Her mouth formed an "o." She grabbed a blanket draped over the arm of the couch and shoved it beneath him, then pressed on the wound. Ridge screamed, almost blacking out.

"Do you know what you're doing?" Ridge choked out.

Isobelle swallowed. "I've read about through-and-through gunshot wounds."

His mouth quirked. "Of course you did."

Tears rolled down her cheeks. "There's so much blood." Then she glared at him. "That was stupid and completely irresponsible! How dare you let him shoot you. You should know better than to be so careless."

"What do you mean?" he panted between breaths. "How else was I going to get you to rip my clothes off?"

Isobelle's laugh turned into a sob. That's when he noticed a small cut on her temple.

"You're hurt."

She looked at him, her expression incredulous. "Me? You're shot!"

Ridge tried to think back. Milton hadn't touched her. "Did... did I do that? When I pushed you?" He reached for her face, gritting again the pain that ripped through him. It was worth it to touch her.

"It's fine, it's nothing," she insisted.

"It's not nothing," he whispered. "I'm so sorry I hurt you."

She pressed her face into his palm for a moment, then

91

shook her head. "You saved my life, you idiot," she whispered, repositioning her hands to put more pressure on his wound.

He coughed and the pain made his eyes water so he closed them. "Worth it." The words slipped out before he could stop them.

Sirens wailed in the distance, drawing close and fast.

Darkness danced along the edges of Ridge's vision but he fought against it. There was something he had to tell Isobelle.

"It was *'Between Sun and Shadow.'*"

Isobelle stilled, her eyes meeting his.

"The first book I left you."

A tear slipped down her cheek. "I wished it was you. Every time Milton said they were from him, I wished it was you." She blinked and more tears fell. "I should have known."

His eyebrows lifted. At least that didn't hurt. "Izzy, I'm so sorry. I should have said—"

"No, no." She shook her head. "They meant so much and I was so overwhelmed with Dad and the fire I just didn't..." She looked at him again. "I'm so sorry, Ridge."

His eyelids grew heavy, which made him angry. He wanted to look at her, to not let her out of his sight. Ridge let them drift shut, trying to refocus.

"Don't." Isobelle's harsh voice snapped them back open. "Don't you dare close your eyes. Just look at me. Stay with me or I swear I'll slap you."

Ridge smiled, not wanting to admit he wasn't going to pass out. "Promise?"

Then there was shouting and pounding footsteps. So many voices. Ridge groaned. Why were they so loud?

A moment later, Isobelle was replaced by a serious-looking woman in a dark medic uniform. She fired off questions while her partner inspected the wound, but Ridge just wanted to see Isobelle again. There were so many people. So much noise.

"Izzy?" he croaked out as an oxygen mask was slipped over his face. The next several minutes were a pain-filled blur as they tried to stem the bleeding. The paramedic said something about a possible liver laceration into the radio on her shoulder. Ridge tried to pull down the mask but his hand was pushed away.

Soon he was being wheeled out, his head light and his eyes struggling to focus. Just as they were about to load him into the ambulance, he thought he caught sight of brown hair.

This time he did pull the mask away. "Izzy," he called, but his voice was weak and she was gone. Frustrated, he lay his head back down and said to the night sky, "I love you. I always have."

Thirteen

Beep. Beep. Beep.

Ridge winced as the sound pushed through the fog surrounding his brain. He was so tired and that sound really needed to stop. He tried to pry open his eyes. It took far more effort than it should have.

A dull, gray ceiling stared back at him and he blinked over and over. When he tried to roll over, a searing pain sliced through him and he groaned.

"Well," said a voice he would recognize anywhere, "it's about time you woke up. Most of us are busy and don't have time to sit around watching yo'ass sleep all day."

Vic stepped into view but Ridge had to blink a few more times before he came into focus.

Ridge licked his lips. "Who let you in here?"

"You did," Vic said. "You need more friends if you're desperate enough to make me your emergency contact."

Ridge kind of smiled. "You're not exactly the face

men dream of seeing when they wake up from a nap." The words came out in a scratchy whisper.

Vic hooted. "You call hours of surgery and recovery a nap? Besides" —he waved at his face— "this is a thing of beauty."

Ridge smiled as the old man sat in a chair that was pulled close to his bed.

"Surgery?" Ridge asked.

"You don't remember?" Vic leaned back. "You lost a lot of blood. The bullet nicked your liver. If that girl of yours hadn't called the police when she had or hadn't been there to keep pressure on your wound, we might have lost you."

Ridge didn't miss the crack in the old man's voice.

Clearing his throat, Vic added. "Not that anyone would miss your ugly mug." He sniffed and looked away.

"Isobelle?" Ridge asked. "Has she..." He swallowed. "Is she alright?"

Vic nodded. "She's been through a lot, but she's strong. She's been dividing her time between you and her father."

That made Ridge's heart speed up. Vic glanced at the heart monitor and smiled.

"Turns out," Vic went on, "that Freewater fellow had been paying off a nurse to overmedicate the old man to keep him here while he worked on your girl. The guy's in rough shape but the doc thinks he'll pull through."

Ridge closed his eyes for a moment. "Milton. I can't believe I killed him." As much as he didn't like the guy, he never wanted his death.

"You didn't."

Eyes snapping open, Ridge turned to Vic, his breath coming out in a rush. "What?"

"It was close and he's in a coma, but he's not dead. If he wakes up, he has a lot to answer for."

Ridge took that in for a moment, a weight lifting away. He hadn't killed anyone. "Wait, what do you mean he has a lot to answer for?"

"Before the Freewater lawyers hedged things up, the police were able to uncover that Milton was illegally tracking Isobelle's phone. They also found all his plans for a new waterfront casino complete with resorts, country clubs, a golf course... you name it."

Ridge nodded. "Milton admitted as much. That would have changed everything about this town."

"Oh yes," Vic agreed. "Especially since it was to be a front for a drug business. Freewater owed a lot of money to a gang looking to expand its territory."

This news made Ridge want to climb out of bed and punch the guy again, coma or no coma.

"But enough about that," Vic said. "Let's talk about your girl." His dark eyes sparkled. "I like her."

Ridged coughed and grimaced as needles of fire shot through him. "She's not *my* girl."

"And who's fault is that?" Vic asked, raising an eyebrow like he always did when Ridge did something wrong. "Listen, life is too short. That should be abundantly clear to you. Don't waste it. Tell her how you feel."

Ridge just sighed, too tired to argue.

Vic shook his head. "You young folk need to learn how to communicate. Just talk to her. Quit making things so damn complicated."

Ridge drew in a slow breath. "Really? And when were you going to communicate that you had cancer?"

Vic scowled. "You were snoopin' in my private business?"

Ridge glared back, refusing to feel bad about it.

Vic threw up his hands. "The doc said the cancer was too widespread. It was a terminal diagnosis."

Terminal. For a moment, Ridge felt like he'd been shot again.

Vic shrugged. "Doc said chemo might give me a few more months but..." He looked at his hands. "I'm tired, Ridge. I miss my family."

Maybe it was the pain meds or the fact that he almost died, but an ache filled Ridge's throat and his eyes burned. "You—you can't.... You are *my* family. I want those few more months." He swallowed hard. "I don't know what I would've done without you. You saved me."

Vic was quiet for so long Ridge started to think maybe he shouldn't have said that.

Then, the old man's dark, calloused hand slipped over his own and squeezed. "You are the only thing I regret leaving behind."

A tear slipped down Ridge's face.

"*You* saved me, my boy. That day I saw you in the grocery store, dirty and beaten, you saved me. Gave me purpose. I didn't think I would ever love anyone again."

Another stupid tear.

"I would be proud to call you my son," Vic said, his voice finally breaking.

Ridge closed his eyes as the tears flowed now and

squeezed Vic's hand back. "I would be proud to call you my father," he whispered.

His phone buzzed and Vic glanced at it, clearing his throat.. "It's your mom again."

"My mom?"

Vic handed it to him. "She's been calling since they told her you were out of surgery."

Ridge swallowed. It had been weeks since they'd spoken. He pushed the answer button.

"Hello?"

"Ridge? Oh, thank heavens you're finally awake."

He heard her sniff and an awkward silence fell.

"How are you?" he finally asked.

His mom took a bit to answer. "I'm... it's hard, but I think I'm glad to be here. I've realized I need to be here."

"That's good," he said.

"Listen, Ridge, I won't keep you but I just wanted to say I love you and I'm glad you're alright. And... and I'm so very sorry." Soft sobs followed her words.

Ridge closed his eyes, feeling a sense of peace settled over him. Man, he should get shot more often. "It's okay, Mom. Just get better."

"Okay," she said. "You too. I'll call you later."

"Yeah. Oh, and Mom?" Ridge gripped the phone. "I love you too."

The next time Ridge opened his eyes, Vic was gone and Isobelle sat in the chair beside his bed, reading a book. He watched her silently, tracing every line of her features with his eyes, touching her skin with his gaze.

As though sensing it, she looked up. He offered a small smile. She closed the book and leaned forward.

"Hi," she said, softly.

"Hi."

They sat like that for a moment while Isobelle's thumb traced circles over the skin of his hand.

"That must be a new one," he mumbled.

"What?"

He pointed to the book on the stand beside his bed. "I don't recognize it."

"Oh. Yeah." She smiled. "I think you would like it."

He searched her face, noting the small red mark there from when he pushed her. "Are you okay? Vic told me about your father. I'm sorry."

Isobelle let out a slow breath. "It'll take some time, but he'll be alright." Then her chin quivered and she looked away. "Ridge, I'm so sorry. I'm so so sorry—"

"Hey," he cut in. "It's not your fault."

Isobelle just shook her head. "If I hadn't been such an idiot, I would have paid more attention to the red flags."

"Well, that's true," Ridge agreed. "The yellow car and the BEAST license plate should have been a dead give-away to stay away from that guy."

She huffed out a laugh. "Yeah."

"Why did you like him?" Ridge asked, genuinely curious.

She shrugged. "He was actually quite nice at first, charming even. And if I'm being honest, well, it was all so grand. Flying me to Paris for the weekend or to another state just to go to a restaurant he liked. It all seemed so romantic, like something straight out of a book." Shaking her head, she scooted closer to the bed, and when she looked at him again, her whole face had crumpled. "You almost died. I was so stupid! I'm so, so sorry."

Ridge reached out and took her arm, giving it a tug, ignoring the pain that shot through him. Isobelle let him pull her into his arms, and she lay half bent over the bed with her head tucked under his chin. He held her while she cried.

Ridge thought of Vic and what he'd said about not wasting time.

"I would do it again if it meant saving you," he whispered.

They stayed like that for a long time and for the first time in years, the deep, painful ache in his chest that had been a constant in his life since childhood loosed just a bit.

"Did you know, I had the biggest crush on you when we were kids?" she asked.

"You did?" He felt her nod against his chest.

"Remember that day I tried to pick a rose but fell into the bush? So you got one down for me?"

Ridge's mouth lifted on one side. "I remember."

"You were my hero," she laughed. "But I was too shy to say anything. Then things got rough with your parents and I didn't know what to do. By the time we were in high school…"

Ridge felt her shrug.

"You were so popular. Everyone liked you and I was just a bookworm. How was I supposed to compete with all those pretty girls wanting your attention? Why would you be interested in me?"

Ridge still didn't say anything. The shock of it all sent

his mind racing back through so many memories. Does she really not know how beautiful she is? How had he not known about her feelings? Or... maybe he just hadn't noticed. He remembered the way she'd smiled up at him when he'd given her the rose, the look on her face when she caught him flirting with all the girls, but there were other things too.

Her laugh when he told her stories from his trips, the way she listened when he confessed to something terrible about his parents, the way she'd never judged him for how poor he was.

For a while they stayed like that, swapping stories back and forth, laughing over incidents from long ago, each sharing their side of the same story.

Ridge pressed her to him, his heart warm. Isobelle lifted her head and rested her chin in her hands, searching his eyes. Her face was so close and a familiar yearning filled Ridge. His hand twitched, wishing he could run a thumb over her lips.

"Did you mean what you said?" she finally asked.

Ridge scrunched his face. "When?"

She looked down for a moment, drew in a deep breath, then met his eyes. "Right before they stuck you in the ambulance, you said you loved me, that you always had."

The beeping on the heart monitor sped up again and Ridge swallowed hard. *Traitor.* His throat was so dry.

"Every word."

Isobelle smiled, then, wide and true. "Then kiss me already. I've waited far too long."

Ridge's eyebrows shot up as she closed the gap between them.

"I've waited my whole life," he whispered.

Her hand ran down the side of his face and he closed his eyes and tried to just... breathe. "Am I pretty drugged up? I'm not hallucinating, am I?"

Isobelle laughed. Ridge still didn't open his eyes, convinced he was dreaming, but then, warm breath brushed his skin and scented heat pushed away the smell of cleaning alcohol.

He opened his eyes. She was so close, her brown eyes wide and wanting.

"Kiss me."

His heart pulsed hard against his ribs. Despite the pain, Ridge lifted a hand to her face, and slid it back behind her head. "You don't have to tell me twice." Then, he pulled her to him.

Their lips touched, and fire shot through his veins. Isobelle pulled back like she felt it too and met his gaze with wide eyes. Ridge didn't move, afraid he'd upset her. But then, she smiled and leaned back in. This time, her mouth opened to meet his and she leaned into it, her hands grasping his face.

Ridge's heart burst. All those years of waiting, yearning, wanting, needing. He sighed as her hand slid into his hair. This moment was everything.

Fourteen

Four months later, Ridge stepped into Vic's gym. He breathed in the stale scent of sweat and vinyl mats. It was quiet without the grunts and calls of men and women sparring or punching.

He ran his fingers over the old desk that held the computer where members checked in, then stopped to look at all the photos on the wall. Vic with a champion boxer, Vic with a group of teens that had gone through his summer program. Vic with—him.

Ridge stared. He'd never seen this photo before. He wasn't even sure how long it had hung there. Carefully, he lifted it from the nail. It was a candid shot of Vic on one knee, a hand resting on the shoulder of a young Ridge, whose head hung low, defeat evident in his shoulders.

He swallowed, clearly remembering that moment. Mom hadn't come out of her room in over a week and some kids had stolen his lunch at school. He'd been so hungry he could barely punch anything and had dropped, feeling defeated. Vic had come over, knelt down and started in on one of his famous tough love lectures, but then Ridge's stomach had growled. The old man stopped mid-sentence and just looked at him. Finally he stood and said, "Follow me."

That was the day Vic started feeding him in exchange for some light cleaning chores. Ridge remembered feeling grateful it hadn't been offered as charity.

He flipped the frame over and froze. Written on the back in Vic's handwriting it said, "The day I became a father again."

Ridge pulled in a slow breath, blinking hard and fast. "I miss you, you stubborn old man."

Carefully, he hung the frame back up.

"Ridge?"

Isobelle's voice floated through the gym door and he turned. As much as he hated that they were both in black, he couldn't deny she was absolutely stunning in it. Her long brown hair had been left loose and flowed down her back. He never got tired of seeing her, of holding her.

He rubbed his chest. Why did everything have to build up so tightly there? Both the good and the bad, always fighting for the same space?

She saw him and smiled. "Hey."

He smiled back.

Isobelle had visited the gym many times with him, especially over the last month while Vic had helped him to slowly work back into rebuilding the strength he had lost.

She wrapped her arms around him, resting her head on his chest. "You okay?"

Ridge closed his eyes, letting her body mold to his. "I just can't believe he's gone. It was too fast. I wasn't ready."

"I don't know that anyone can ever be ready for this kind of loss."

"I miss him already," Ridge whispered.

Isobelle just held him. "I know."

Finally, he drew in a deep breath and pulled back slightly. "And I still can't believe he left me all this."

Isobelle looked around. "He knew you loved the gym like he did and that you would take care of it."

Ridge did love it and he would do everything in his power to keep it in top shape, just like Vic would expect him to. But all the money? Ridge shook his head. He had no idea Vic had put away so much, or had invested so wisely. The old man was still full of surprises, even after he was gone.

He gripped Isobelle's hand and moved toward the door. "Do you want to swing by the bookstore on the way back?"

Her face split into a huge smile, making Ridge's heart flip. "Yes, please! Oh, and just so you know, I decided to go with the more expensive crown molding." Her expression was smug. "I figure if the Freewater fortune is paying for everything, why not go with the very best."

Ridge laughed, feeling the faint ache in his gut from the bullet wound. "A very wise choice." He kissed her nose. "Do you think they'll have it done in time for Gabrielle's visit?"

Isobelle clasped her hands together. "The contractor said he only needed a few more days." She sighed, sounding blissfully content. "I still can't believe she's willing to travel out here just for my grand opening, and with a whole box of her signed books!"

Ridge was glad the author had been so kind and gracious when she'd heard about the fire. He would have to personally thank her for making Isobelle so happy.

The new bookstore was three times the size of the original one, complete with a kid's section and small coffee shop. The Freewater board of directors had insisted on paying for everything and then some to compensate for all the damages Milton had caused.

After Milton had come out of the coma, he'd been sent to a mental institution to finish out his recovery before charges were pressed.

Isobelle was practically floating on air by the time they'd finished walking through the nearly completed bookshop.

"Oh," Isobelle said. "What's that?" She pointed to a book set on a table in the middle of the store. She went over and picked it up. Ridge wiped his hands on his suit, watching her face as she opened the book. Petals fell from the pages and she drew in a sharp breath.

She looked up, meeting his eyes. Between her fingers she held the ring he'd placed inside.

"I hope it's not terrible timing," Ridge mumbled, his skin suddenly hot. "But when I spoke to Vic about it, he requested I ask you on the day of his funeral. He didn't want it to be a sad day. I hope you don't mind—"

Isobelle placed a finger on his lips, halting the onslaught of words.

Her smile reached her eyes. "It's perfect." Then she

kissed him. Ridge pulled her tighter, drinking in everything about her.

He pulled back to catch his breath. "Does that mean yes?"

Isobelle laughed. "Yes! A thousand times, yes."

Then, she kissed him again and Ridge couldn't wait to do it forever.

THE END

About the Author

Serene Heiner is the creative soul behind the growing Instagram and TikTok accounts @magicalbooknook. When she's not writing, drawing, sewing, taking book photos, making videos, or crafting, (deep breath) she can be found either participating in her workout group or training for her next Spartan race. Serene is a diehard fantasy reader but can be caught cheating on the genre from time to time. She's a proud mother to seven little readers and lives with them and her husband in their home in Idaho where books are stacked to the ceiling. Where does she find the time to write? The world may never know.

Instagram TikTok